The King and the Widow

One Thousand and One Camels

Emile Tubiana

 Published by Le Pont International, Ltd.

BOOKS BY THE SAME AUTHOR

L'enfance gagnée (French)
Balance (English)
The Spider's Web (English)
Les trésors cachés (French)

Cover art and design: Viviane Tubiana

First Edition: February 2014

ISBN: 0991448804
ISBN-13: 978-0-9914488-0-7

Contents

Characters

Harun Al-Rashid	King of Persia and Caliph of Baghdad
General Omar	Harun Al-Rashid's Chief of Staff
Farah, called Farha	Harun Al-Rashids second wife
Khayet	Harun Al-Rashid and Farha's daughter
Zaafer Lebranki	Harun Al-Rashid's *Wazir* (minister)
Saad (Lucky)	Jewish storyteller from Jerusalem
Abed	Rich merchant
Omra	Abed's wife
Amir	Abed and Omra's son
Rabha	Abed's friend's daughter
Soraya	The widow
Bousid El Hallali	General Omar's son
Rahman	Soraya's son
Colonel Rabiya	General Omar's most reliable man
Barka	Rabiya's sister
Leila	Soraya's sister
Farida	Bousid's wife
Yahya	Zaafer Lebranki's father
Mokhtar	Bousid's son
Naziha	Zaafer Lebranki's daughter
Aziza	Mokhtar's first wife
Jamil	Bousid's friend

Preface

When I was a child at the age of ten, most of Tunisia was under German occupation. Our house was damaged by the German bombs. We fled about twenty miles away from our town and finally landed on a French farm, together with many other refugees. We were placed in a barn with many other families, where we all slept like sardines, one family next to the other. In the evenings, my father would get everyone to stop complaining by telling us one of his stories that would capture the imagination of his audience, just like he used to do it in the time of peace that preceded and succeeded the war.

I had the privilege of always sitting next to my father, when he would tell stories to an audience of family members and neighbors. This way I heard many stories and poems first hand. I was listening carefully, as in school. It was at that time that I began to memorize my father's stories. For this narrative, I selected one of my favorite poems, in loving memory of my father.

Originally, my father told us this story in verses. Based upon these verses, I decided to write a story. All characters and descriptions are purely imaginary, any possible resemblance with actual persons or geographic places is not intentional.

I never knew where the original poem came from. I only know from my mother that she had heard it for the first time from my grandfather.

The title of the poem was, "Elf Naga oo Naga", which means "One Thousand and One Camels."

The story takes place at the end of the eighth century, during the time when Harun Al-Rashid (pronounced *Hārūn ar-Rashīd*) was king of the Persian Empire and caliph of Baghdad. In the stories that were created around his name he was known as a just ruler who cared for his people.

Chapter 1

Farha

Harun Al-Rashid was lying on his sofa when the messenger arrived on his horse and brought him a secret message from his chief of staff, General Omar, who was fighting the Byzantines near Damascus. The message was written in Persian and said, "Your Majesty, you are victorious!" Then the message read further, "The Byzantine army belongs to the past."

A few hours earlier, Harun Al-Rashid had been sad and anxious to know the news, but while reading this message from General Omar, he smiled. No one knew the reason for this sudden smile. His closest adviser, who had been gloomy and silent, smiled too, and everyone who sat in that room smiled at that moment for the first time since the king had retreated to his quarters for a few days, awaiting the news from General Omar who was on the front. He strongly feared the Byzantines, who could have put an end to his reign and to his empire, and now General Omar announced their defeat. No one knew the

reason for the king's mood change, but it gave his entourage a wind of hope.

Since that time, General Omar was his most trusted man and he enjoyed a lot of privileges. The general's staff, who helped him against this terrible enemy, stayed loyal to its military commander, and was rewarded with many advantages and perks. The mere fact that an officer was able to say that he had been with General Omar would earn him much respect and admiration as a national hero.

This scene occurred years before Harun Al-Rashid met his second wife Farah. His first wife had died one year after he had married her, and he didn't have any children from her. It was an arranged marriage of convenience. At that time, his father, who was very ill, introduced a princess from a neighboring country to become Harun's wife. Harun Al-Rashid was very worried about his father's health. He didn't want to disappoint him, as he cared for him, and as he had no feelings for his first wife, he just obeyed his father. He spent a few years as a widower before he found another woman, this time according to his choice.

One day, he was traveling in his coach surrounded by a dozen of his best security guards. Before dusk, his advisor suggested they make a stop in order to find a convenient place to spend the night. While his advisor and two of his guards were searching for a suitable place,

they left the king with the remaining guards not far from a well and from an elegant house, which seemed to be the home of a well-to-do family. The king wished to ask for fresh water to quench his thirst and relax his legs. No one could guess that it was the king who was in the coach. He purposely never traveled with his royal clothes, in order to avoid curiosity and all kinds of trouble. When Harun knocked at the door, a well-dressed man opened it. The king looked at the nice house and suddenly he saw a young and lovely lady who was not far from the door. At first he was surprised to see such a beautiful and elegant lady who spoke with kindness while addressing the servant who opened the door. She seemed not to have any fear of strangers, as she saw the guards who were surrounding the house and didn't give them any thought. She was smart and polite. Her eyes captivated the king while she was talking to the servant. Her father, who saw the guards from the window, came to the door and asked the servant, "Do you need any help?" Then he addressed the king, to know whether he needed anything.

Without revealing his identity, the king answered, "Thank you Sir, your servant is very kind. He is taking care of me."

The father, who was curious to find out more, went slowly, slowly towards the door, so he could see the gentleman more closely. When he got very close to the

door, he suddenly saw the golden ring on the finger of this man. He realized that he had to be polite, and then he said, "Do we have the honor of speaking with His Majesty the king?"

The king answered, "You are an intelligent man." The father, without any hesitation, opened the doors wide and bowed. The king was embarrassed and said, "Please, there is no need to bow. After all, you are a kind person." As he was saying this, the lovely lady came back with a ceramic cup and a water jug.

The father interrupted and said to the king, "Please enter." He made a sign to his daughter to let her understand that the guest was His Majesty the king.

She made a sign to the king to follow her. She led him to what looked like a large guest room. The king followed her and discovered that the room was majestic. The king felt comfortable, and he was strongly attracted to the young lady who looked at him with a smile, which was unusual at that time in that region. The young lady looked at the king with astonishment. He looked at her too. He had the feeling that he had known her for a long time. The king politely asked her name. She answered with a very nice voice, "My name is Farah."

The king had fallen in love with her from the first moment he had seen her. He loved her so much that he did not take a long time to marry her. Farah was the ideal woman, and she had all the good qualities to be a queen,

although she was of common origin. The king was eager to please her; he even had a new castle built in her honor next to the new city of Baghdad. He gave her the name Farha, which means "joy". Two years after their wedding, she gave birth to a beautiful daughter, who resembled her mother like two drops of dew. They called her Khayet, which means "Life". The kindness of his wife and the loveliness of his daughter made him so happy that it reflected on his attitude toward his servants and his entourage.

Harun Al-Rashid was so preoccupied with his wife and daughter that he neglected the empire's business and ceased to project strength. His advisors feared that his kindness and his distraction might be interpreted as weakness. His enemies could soon start challenging his power, and the empire could be shaking. They looked to his wife as the main reason for his change in mood and for influencing his decisions. When his daughter was about ten years old, his advisors plotted against the queen, and with the help of her ladies-in-waiting they succeeded in slowly getting rid of her. When she came down with an illness, they saw to it that she was not properly cared for, until she was so weak that no healer could help her anymore.

During his wife's illness, the king was constantly absent. He neglected his duties and everything was decided by his *wazir*, who was in fact the secretary of

both interior and exterior affairs. The *wazir* was both his right hand and closest advisor and, as the king never had a friend, the *wazir* filled this gap. The name of the *wazir* was Zaafer Lebranki. It came to the point that Harun Al-Rashid did not make any decisions without first consulting Zaafer Lebranki. He didn't mind letting the power escape his hands as long as he could watch over his wife's frail health. He had brought wise healers from all the corners of his empire, but his wife's condition did not improve.

Chapter 2

The King's Sorrow

After two years of illness, the queen died. The king was totally devastated. His entourage was happy to lose her, as everyone thought that she didn't belong in the palace. Farah had been an open-minded woman who was not afraid to say what she had on her mind. This was the reason why Zaafer Lebranki didn't like her, and he made sure that no one in his entourage dared challenge him. The queen was so smart, she knew why he didn't like her - he always wanted the king to follow his advice and not hers.

The burial ceremony went unnoticed, but the princes and princesses from all the provinces, and many crowned heads from other countries, came to express their condolences. They especially wanted to be seen at the court, but the caliph did not pay any attention to the visitors. Zaafer Lebranki, on the other hand, took advantage of their presence to negotiate with them and to strengthen the empire. Zaafer Lebranki took care of the affairs of the state, and he never let anyone notice the king's constant absence.

Never before had such a small and newly built city as Baghdad seen so many beautiful young ladies. The king's palace was between the foothills of the Persian mountains and Baghdad. The visitors came from many corners of the empire. Everyone was hoping to be seen by the newly widowed caliph.

Needless to say, his heart was full of grief, and he hardly noticed the presence of the distinguished ladies who were visiting. He never forgot that he had vowed in his heart, at his wife's tomb never to marry again. Farah was the only woman who filled his life with joy and happiness. She was fair and outspoken, while all other women were obedient and never dared ask any questions. Farah used to laugh with him many times; she said things that no one dared say, not even his closest adviser. She had been of a good and kind nature and was easy-going and even-tempered. Her self-confidence was appropriate for and worthy of a queen. She brought youth and cheer to the palace. Harun Al-Rashid, who was not young anymore, felt rejuvenated by her presence; that was the reason for giving her the name of Farha, which also means "cheer" in Arabic. In her passing she took with her the cheer he had known. Harun Al-Rashid avoided any talk or any communication with the palace servants. Only his oldest servant was able to talk with him.

In the meantime, Zaafer Lebranki, who didn't know anything about the caliph's vow, was trying to find an appropriate lady to replace the late queen. He was looking for a woman who could be a friend and a wife to the king. His conditions were that the new queen would be submissive to him and that her family would give him a financial advantage.

In order to make a selection, Zaafer Lebranki organized a feast and invited most of the princesses from the neighboring countries to enable the king to receive them and to choose the right one. For his guest list he made sure to first include the princesses whose families he knew already. The reception hall was richly decorated with drapes and rugs from near and far. Many princesses came with their ladies-in-waiting. The *wazir* knew almost every princess. Many were nice and beautiful; some were not. He knew very well that some would not please the king, but he wanted a large selection to pick from. Caravans of camels and horses from many places filled the city. They bore all kinds of goods: finest silk from China, rugs from India and from Marrakesh and Kairouan in North Africa, and precious stones and jewelry from Africa. Hundreds of animals - cows, sheep, goats, and chickens streamed in all year long. There were gifts from other countries and from other regions of the empire. This was an occasion to be noticed by the king. Every princess kept her hope alive. No one knew the real state of mind of the king.

During the festivities the king did not react to any of the lovely princesses who came to the palace. The *wazir* was unhappy and attributed the king's attitude to temporary sadness, due to the loss of his wife. Harun Al-Rashid was polite and behaved well toward the guests. Once the princesses and their families had left the palace, the *wazir* felt sad, as the festivity room was empty, and Harun Al-Rashid became more heavy-hearted. For thirty days he did not leave his palace. The only persons who had access to him were his lovely daughter Khayet and her maid. Even Zaafer Lebranki and General Omar could see him only on rare occasions. Many delegations visited the king just to get a chance to arrange a marriage for him. Every princess hoped to marry this great king. This was a unique opportunity to present a nice woman to the king. Everyone wanted the privilege of being connected with the king's family and of having direct access to the palace. That year very few weddings were performed, as every princess kept the dream alive of becoming Al-Rashid's wife.

The financial situation of the empire had greatly improved, but the king ignored all these treasures. He spent most of the time with his daughter. Zaafer Lebranki announced every new present, just to find out what his reaction would be. The king tried to keep himself in a relatively cheerful mood, but when night neared he fell back into sorrow, he was as sad as on the day his wife passed away. No one could make him change his mood.

He couldn't sleep anymore. His advisers and his servants were concerned about the state of his health. They had brought all kinds of comedians, who tried in vain to lift his mood. Al-Rashid was not even watching or paying attention. The comedians, who had always electrified the courtiers, also seemed gloomy for failing to cheer up the king. All efforts were to no avail. All the eyes of the courtiers were set upon Al-Rashid. His face didn't show any sign of enthusiasm. He was silent, and his eyes were directed to nowhere. He looked like someone who was dreaming. No one knew what he was thinking.

His closest friend and advisor, Zaafer Lebranki, didn't know what to do for his king. He tried everything possible, but everything was in vain. Finally, he remembered the Jewish storyteller from Jerusalem, who had many times made the king and his deceased wife laugh like children.

Chapter 3

The Storyteller

One day, the king's storyteller from Jerusalem, who was well known to the king and whom he had liked very much in the past, was finally ordered to come to the king's court. He was an old Jewish man, whose name was Saad, which means "lucky". He was from an old religious Jewish tribe. His name was known in the entire empire from the Mediterranean Sea in the west, to Asia Minor in the north, to the Nile and all the way between the Nile and the Indian Ocean in the south, and to India in the east. He had the reputation of being the best storyteller. He was very discreet and was respected in every palace. His stories were appreciated, as they were full of wisdom. He knew many of the languages spoken in that area. This was also one of the reasons why every king welcomed him. The noble and rich families liked him, as he had access to every king's court. His knowledge, art, character and trustworthiness earned him respect and honor. The kings liked to listen to his stories and some of his advice. He had saved the life of many persons who were in trouble with the authorities.

His family lived in Jerusalem enjoying a good life and security. No king or caliph could afford not to listen to his advice or his stories. His schedule was prepared by a good secretary and booked almost a year in advance. Zaafer Lebranki had to send a courier to Jerusalem to invite him for one evening. The message was formulated as follows, "Honorable Mr. Saad, Harun Al-Rashid needs you urgently, please come for the end of this month." When Saad read the message he understood that he had to go. Although another king had booked him for that time, he knew well that no one would be upset, as Harun Al-Rashid was the strongest king in the region. Saad left Jerusalem a week after the messenger left with his confirmation. As soon as he received the word from Saad, Zaafer Lebranki sent out couriers with invitations to the guests. In the palace everyone awaited Saad's arrival with great expectation and hope.

It took more than a week from Jerusalem to Baghdad; the long journey was tiring and he had to pass many hurdles. His caravan had to go through the desert and cross a few dangerous rivers to reach Baghdad. The caravan was composed of horses and donkeys and was protected by a platoon from the Tuvia family, which was recognized since the time of the Romans as the most reliable security guards for the safety of merchant caravans going to every part of the Middle East. His staff comprised twenty people who helped him in his mission. When Saad reached the palace, he entered the king's

courtyard with his caravan, which carried him and his servants. His rabbi accompanied him everywhere, as Saad was a religious and observant man. The donkeys with all their belongings were part of the caravan.

Saad's arrival alerted Zaafer and the guards, who were well prepared and waiting for this moment with great expectation. This time Saad noticed that he was receiving a greater welcome than ever before. He didn't know the reason, but, as usual, he didn't bother to inquire. Saad was patient and said to himself, as was his custom, *We will know at the right time.* The inhabitants of the palace were waiting for him. Saad didn't pay much attention to this special reception that was ordered for him. Saad was used to being received with acclaim and fanfare. They gave him all the honors usually reserved only for royal dignitaries. He was assigned guest quarters in the king's palace and received at his disposal servants, a kosher cook, a masseur who took care of him, and one of the king's equerries and his helpers, who took care of his horses, of his donkeys, and of his huge trunks.

Saad brought with him a large wardrobe, as he never knew how long the trip would last and what kind of dignitaries he might encounter. He wanted to be ready for every occasion and always feel at ease. When he arrived, his clothes were covered with dust from the journey. He refreshed himself and changed his clothes. The next day, after a good night's sleep, he wore his silk

gown and ceremonial robes. Then he savored some fruit brought to him by the servants. After that he closed the door to prepare himself quietly for the nightly performance. Saad knew the king from the past, but no one had told him about the king's new condition and the passing of the queen. Only a few people in the king's closest entourage were informed about his actual state of mind.

In the evening the large hall was slowly, slowly filling up with dignitaries from many neighboring countries. Every one of the guests was patiently awaiting Harun Al-Rashid's arrival. They were eager to see him after such an extended absence from the public eye. The princesses had come mainly to see and to be seen by the widowed king. Now and again the audience stood up to greet a well-known dignitary as he entered the hall. Many knew Saad from his various performances. When the king was about to approach the door, they signaled Saad to enter first. He entered through the large interior door of the reception hall. The room was decorated with rugs from every major province; this created a magnificent festive atmosphere. After a while, the king finally appeared, and the sound of the applause produced a sense of solemnity. Saad welcomed the king with a faint smile. As he tried to kiss his hand, as custom required, the king reacted immediately with a gesture and said, "My dear Saad, I have missed you, and I have missed your stories."

Saad smiled graciously and responded, "Your Majesty, it is an immense honor for me to be called again to your royal palace, and it will give me great pleasure to share my favorite story with you and your guests." The king smiled for the first time since his wife had passed away. A wind of life blew into the king's soul. His face lit-up, and the guests sensed this new air.

"Harun Al-Rashid is alive and well", said Zaafer Lebranki loudly. The king seemed to have been resuscitated.

His entourage praised him with applause, "God bless our king and caliph of Baghdad Harun Al-Rashid! God bless our king Harun Al-Rashid!"

The king greeted his entourage. Then he called Saad to sit next to him, which was not usual in that part of the world, but he wanted to give special attention to his guest, according to the Muslim custom. He chatted a while with him, then he let him go to his place. Saad's small stage was made up of a white chair, which was draped with red silk. It was on the other side of the hall, facing the king's throne, and was ready for the storyteller.

The noise from the audience was suddenly cut short. The king had just made a sign to Saad to sit down. Then another signal. This time, with a blink of his eye. The splendid room was now entirely quiet. One could sense that the noise in the air had come to a sudden halt. A

complete silence took over. The guests waited for Saad to commence. The king's face brightened up. He remembered Saad from the time when his wife was still alive. Saad too recalled clearly the royal couple when he was here for the last time, and he remembered the charming queen. This time she was missing, but Saad didn't say anything, as he did not know whether the queen was late or absent. Contrary to the Muslim custom the king's daughter Khayet sat next to Harun Al-Rashid. Khayet's presence did not escape Saad's furtive glance. The princess was a gracious and charming hostess. Many princes and princesses were invited for this unique event. The guests' eyes were directed towards the king and his lovely daughter. Khayet was so well dressed and had such a wonderful and elegant appearance that one might have thought that she was the queen. She looked like her mother. Saad was making a few small moves to attract the audience's attention. He was comparable to a violinist, tuning his violin. Then he picked up the glass of water next to him, took a sip, and adjusted his position on the chair to feel more comfortable for the evening. Once he felt at ease, he moved his head, first towards the king, then he looked to the right, then to the left, and then he spoke with a soft but firm tone as he looked at the special and magnificent audience, which was dressed up for the occasion. He said, "Your Majesty, and honorable guests...." At the same moment a flow of servants in red silk turbans entered the hall, streaming from many

directions. Each one was holding a tray filled with nuts and dates. They were followed by a parade of servants with white turbans, each one holding a teapot and a tray with cakes dipped in honey. The room was tumultuous again. Saad smiled politely towards the servants, as if to say, "It is all right, do what you have to do." He had stopped short, but this was part of Saad's way of performing. With the permission of the king he liked to master and to orchestrate every action in the room during his performance. This way he avoided any surprise, or any wrong action from anyone in the room, which might have interfered with his story. He always consulted the king's court as to how everything should be handled. He himself timed each sequence of the evening. He let everyone enjoy their tea and his dessert quietly. Of course, the guests exchanged words among themselves, which created some uproar. Once everyone was served, Saad winked to the chief servant. The latter was dressed in baggy white silk breeches, and his waist was wrapped with a large red belt made out of a special red felt. He stood at the wide entrance to the room like an officer supervising the servants' movements and actions. With his simple wink all the servants disappeared as quickly as they arrived. The king relished this small intermission as he enjoyed seeing his servants offering his guests delicacies. Then Saad cleared his throat in a way that everyone could hear him. He smiled furtively towards the king and continued, "What a great evening we are

having!" Like a magician, he waved his hand. Suddenly, twenty young belly dancers appeared with the bowed *rebab* (fiddle), the flute and the *tam tam* (drum) players. The sound of the oriental instruments created an extraordinary atmosphere. The pulsating rhythm of the music and the belly dancers filled the hall. The entire audience seemed pleased and enjoyed the rhythm. The king moved his eyes from left to right. The sound of the music seemed to distract him. Khayet was very happy to see her father in a better mood. She glanced toward the guests. The young princes looked happy to see Khayet in a good mood, and everyone tried to stand out in order to attract her attention. She was cheerful and had created a festive ambiance among the princes and princesses. Saad too was sipping tea once in a while. He was used to such splendid evenings; it was his job and his art to make people happy. He kept greeting the dignitaries with a simple and gracious movement of his hand and his head. He mastered the art of making everyone feel unique and special. This was one of the reasons he was beloved by all.

The marvelous hall was set this way: the men were sitting on one side and the women were sitting in an adjacent room. The women's room was connected with the main room. The separating wall was half height. There were no panels on the top, but instead it was draped with a slightly transparent silk veil. The women could see the men, but the men could not clearly

distinguish the women, as it was prescribed by the Islamic rules. They saw only shapes; this was also the custom of the empire. Khayet was an exception. She was sitting with her father, the king. The eyes of all the men and women were directed to her, but she was smart and played her role very well.

Saad had known Farah, the deceased queen, from past appearances. He had met her on a few occasions in her palace. She was young and beautiful. At that time, Farah was the only woman in the palace who dared enter the room where the king was sitting. She was an open-minded queen. She used to question the guests and many times put some dignitaries in an awkward position. The king never rebuked her. He liked the way she spoke with other kings. Sometimes she gave him an edge in his discussion with his counterpart. Saad was very fond of her; she was like one of his daughters. She had always been kind to Saad. He had felt at ease in her presence. Even though he was not a Muslim like her, she had shared many thoughts with Saad that she could not have shared with anyone in the palace. She was broad-minded, which was rare at that time. Saad knew where her family came from. He recalled that one day a dignitary had said to Saad, "Eat the meat, it tastes very good!"

Knowing that Saad would eat only kosher meat, Farah understood the provocation and told the gentleman, "How can you keep your vows to your wife?"

The man was first surprised that the queen had asked such an unusual question, but he nevertheless answered her politely, "Your Royal Highness, that has nothing to do with the meat."

Then she replied, "Our guest Saad made a vow not to eat non-kosher food, and you want him to break his vow and his faith for a piece of meat?" Since that day, the dignitary respected Farah and never dared say anything inappropriate in her presence. At that time in the Persian Empire they trusted Jewish men more than their Muslim subjects to be in the presence of women. Saad was a unique man. He had thoroughly studied the Bible before becoming a storyteller. He had inherited the stories from his father.

The noise in the hall diminished gradually. It seemed that someone had given a signal. Then the king looked to the right, to the left, and finally he looked at Saad who was waiting for his wink. A light breeze came from the two opposite doors. They were opened for a moment, to enable Saad and the guests to breathe some fresh air just before the start. Again a sudden silence cut the noise as if with a sharp knife. This gave the impression that no one was breathing anymore. Saad, with a clear and succinct voice, began with these words, "Once upon a time there was a merchant who lived happily with his wife and his only son. His name was Abed, his wife's name was Omra and his son's name was Amir, which

also means 'prince' in Arabic. His trading business made him rich and famous. His fortune enabled him to live in a very nice house with a garden. He gave his wife and his son a comfortable way of life. Abed's son was still a child when the death of his wife shattered his happiness and his tranquility. His business often took him away from home. By chance he was not traveling when the tragedy occurred. Deep in his heart he thanked God that the death of his wife had not occurred while he was away. Now that his son had become an orphan, he did not want him to suffer from loneliness, especially at his tender age. He loved his wife very much and now he found himself in a large house with his only son. He buried his wife quietly. He tried to spare his son Amir any suffering and sadness. This new situation did not allow him to travel far away from home any longer.

He gave up certain of his business travels and stayed with Amir. This way he could care for him and cherish him all day long. He could not even afford to cry over the loss of his wife in front of anyone for fear of burdening his son. Abed spent many nights in his closed room. He cried for his beloved wife. He felt that he was lucky to have been working all the time and to have saved a lot of money. He could live from his savings for many years to come, and so he spent most of his time with his son. Abed taught the young boy everything, from A to Z. He had to learn how to be a mother to his son. When Amir was old enough to start learning to read

and write, Abed brought a teacher for his son. Over time he hired many knowledgeable people from various fields to teach him, as he sought a princely education for his only son Amir. The young boy first learned the Koran, as it was customary in that region, but he spared his son from becoming a religious man. During the summer Abed, who enjoyed traveling with his son, visited a few of his best customers and friends. He wanted to maintain his good relationships with his fellow merchants. This new life enabled Amir to meet young children of his age.

Each year the son grew taller and smarter; he was well educated and his looks were enhanced by his astuteness. He was also very kind and well behaved. His appearance resembled that of a prince and earned his father many compliments. The trips that Abed provided to his son gave him new experiences. Amir was constantly studying and didn't feel the change of places. Abed made sure that Amir would feel comfortable everywhere. He prepared his son so that he could master any situation that he might encounter in life. He educated his son to behave himself in different levels of society. Amir could play with rich children as well as with poor ones. While his son was still young, Abed refused many invitations from his rich fellow-merchants. He refused many offers to get married again after the passing of his spouse. He could have chosen a new wife, but Abed preferred to stay with his only son.

Once, when Amir had become a young man, Abed accepted an invitation from a famous customer. The host was one of his best merchant friends. He had a splendid house, and his wife was a good friend of Abed's late wife Omra and, fortunately for Amir, they had a daughter of the same age. Her name was Rabha. First, Abed was not sure if he should tell his son about this invitation, or if it would be better to wait until an appropriate occasion would present itself, but during a casual conversation with his son, Abed could not conceal this news about the invitation any longer. Amir was thrilled when he heard that the host had a young girl his age, but he didn't exhibit any enthusiasm to his father. When he went to sleep he tried to visualize the moment when he would encounter her, but he kept pushing this thought away, as it conflicted with the moral education he received. He recalled the day when his father was telling him to be careful with women, but had not explained the meaning of his advice. This thought troubled him and kept him awake. He was very tired from the long day and finally fell asleep. The next day, when his father told him to put on nice clothes, Amir knew in advance that he should wear the best outfit he had, so as to make a good impression. He put on his silk shirt with the robe that his father had bought him on a business trip. He looked so handsome that his father involuntarily kissed him on the cheek. Amir looked at him and said, 'Father, what is this kiss for?' Abed looked at his son and smiled. Amir

understood that this kiss had something to do with his mother. He looked at his father evasively and saw a teardrop on his father's cheek. Then he said, 'Father, are you crying?'

Abed was embarrassed, but he knew that now he could share his feelings with his son, and he responded, 'My son, this gown makes you resemble your mother.'

Amir was touched by this analogy and responded, 'Father, I know that you spent your time with me, giving me great comfort. I know too that you loved my mother.' Abed was pleased with Amir's answer, but he changed the subject quickly as it was time to go to his host's house. When they reached the door, Amir saw something flitter from a small window. The young girl saw Amir and stared at him with a conspicuous smile. But only Amir could discern her smile, and he furtively returned a faint smile, as his father was next to him in the carriage. During dinner Amir found himself facing Rabha at the table, although it was not the custom in that country to have young girls sit at the dinner table with guests. Abed and the host felt that the children were too young to forbid them to be around the table with the grown-ups. Their main concern was to have the children keep each other company, so they could speak together without any distraction. Amir conducted himself exquisitely, and he was thoughtful towards the young girl. He kept his distance, but was attentive and kind to her. He knew well

that this was his father's business relation, and it should not be mixed with any personal feelings.

Father and son had become very close friends and had almost forgotten their common grief. Eventually Abed became accustomed to his life, but his wife's memory was always with him. However, he never showed his son the pain he had been enduring for so many years. Amir had never been left alone with other people, as his father made sure that he was always with him. He had never revealed to his son that he had almost stopped working since his mother passed away. He had spent the money he had laid aside for many years. He never mentioned either that he had to sell some of his property. During their journeys, Amir didn't notice any sign from his father's friends that could have alerted him to the financial situation.

Abed was known to be a wealthy and very honest merchant. He had never had a chance to communicate with his son while his wife was alive. He was always traveling and caring for the family. He strongly sensed the loss of his wife, and the thought of marrying again never occurred to him. He was a good husband and a good father. In the town where he lived the neighbors admired and respected him very much for his decency and gracious manners. His first thought was to have a foreign governess for his son, but he feared the gossip of the people and above all he didn't want his son to

become attached to a stranger. Despite his mother's absence, Amir grew stronger and stronger and became a very desirable young man. His father regularly accompanied him everywhere.

Amir didn't realize that his father's health was not as good as it used to be and that, as the years went by, his fortune diminished from day to day. He had lost a vast amount of money having missed good opportunities and his business was shrinking. Then he became ill as a result of neglecting his own health. He cared so much for his son that anything else became irrelevant. He abstained from seeing any healer for fear of awakening his son's concern. He was certain that he was healthy and resistant to any disease and nothing could happen to him. But deep in his heart and in his mind he wanted to join his beloved wife. He felt that now that his son was a young man and with the education he had given him he could survive in any situation, it was time for him to join his wife.

Amir was very much concerned about his father's well-being. He did whatever he could to help him, but the sickness had made his father very weak.

One day the merchant called his son and told him, 'My son, I am so weak that I believe that my time to depart has arrived.' Then he disclosed all the truth to his son; that he had stopped working as usual, as he wanted to have time with him. 'I wanted you to keep your way

of life unchanged, so you wouldn't miss your mother. My fortune has dwindled to almost nothing. All I have left with me is a ten dinar golden coin.' He moved his heavy body so as to be more comfortable, and then with a deep moan he said, 'I sold our house a long time ago, and the new owner was kind enough to let us stay until today. I owe money to a few friends. The only fortune I still have is this gold coin I just told you about – it's worth just ten dinars and no more – my horse, and the household. I am sorry that I have nothing else to leave you as an inheritance, except this miserable golden coin, but, if you wish, I could give you some advice that in my view may be worth remembering: ***Marry the woman you love, and not for her father's money.*** And, ***Words are more valuable than money.***'

The very next day the father passed away, leaving poor Amir alone with just a ten dinar golden coin. His father's friends were very helpful and took care of the funeral. Everyone was nice to young Amir, but he soon realized that his father owed money to a few of his friends and that he was not able to pay them back. A few days passed since his father's burial. One sunny day he rose with determination and the conviction that his father had wanted to say something important to him, when he told him about his advice. That day he was in a better mood than any other day, and he had a feeling that he would be better off starting a new life somewhere else. After all, he was better educated than any young man of

his age, and at least no one would know about his father's debt.

During the weeks of grieving many of his father's friends visited him and invited him to their houses. Amir never knew that his father had so many friends who loved him. Everyone spoke kindly about his father. They were very helpful to the young man. As Amir was very well behaved, and many of his father's friends who had daughters looked on him as a good candidate for a son-in-law, Amir understood why everyone was generous and kind with him. He knew very well what those friends expected from him instead of the money his father owed them, but he didn't want to fall into a marriage of convenience and remembered well his father's advice. He was also aware that a fortune could make his life much easier and would spare him all the trouble that was waiting for him and for which he was not prepared, but he preferred to follow his father's advice and marry someone he loved.

He remembered well that his father's love for his mother had lasted way after her passing. At that point, he couldn't think about marrying any woman, as he deeply felt the pain of losing his beloved father. He was left alone, his heart filled with emptiness. His father's entire debt did not bother him at all. He knew that while his mother was alive his father had worked hard to give them a good life. After all, his father didn't charge him with

paying back any of his debt, but sooner or later and for his dad's honor he might have to satisfy the creditors.

Amir was well prepared for a high-paying position but hadn't learned any craft to earn his livelihood. Once the weeks of grief and sadness had passed, the new orphan took his courage in his hands and went to the market. There he saw a multitude of merchants who looked at him, some with sympathy and some with curiosity and expectation. A few of the merchants reminded him politely that his father hadn't paid some bill. Amidst the market's clamor, he heard a voice screaming from afar, which said, 'Three words for sale! Only ten dinars!' and then the voice continued, 'Who is the lucky buyer?' The passers-by didn't pay any attention to the man who shouted loudly, as they knew he was a dervish. But for Amir, who was in despair because of the situation he found himself in, the screaming of this man awakened hope in his sore heart. He was also fascinated by the coincidence of the dervish's offer and his father's advice. In this message he saw a sign of his destiny pointing him in the right direction. His father must have known something when he had given him this advice."

Saad interrupted his story to take a sip of water from his glass. At this instance the king looked at him and smiled with relief. No one knew the reason for the smile, and no one could figure out what he had in mind, but

after that evening the king invited Saad for a cup of tea in his living room, and Saad accepted the invitation with pleasure, as not everyone was privileged to be with such a great king who was master of an empire. They spoke about many subjects, particularly about the late queen. When Saad mentioned her name, the king was touched, as he knew that Farah had liked Saad and that he was like a father to her. Then suddenly the king said, "Do you know, Saad, why I was happy and had smiled when you told us about the young Amir's plight in the story? At that time I thought about my daughter, but thank God I possess a fortune and she would not have to fear such a plight as the one Amir was experiencing."

Hearing this, Saad answered, "My king, then you appreciated my story?"

"Yes, yes!" The king answered, and then he continued, "Your story is marvelous." Saad was happy that the king liked his story.

That night, when Saad was telling his story, he paused for a moment, giving the impression that he was coming to something much more exciting than what had been heard up till then; he smiled toward some dignitaries whom he knew well, and continued, "My dear king and honored guests, I was saying that young Amir was so desperate and disoriented that the words of the dervish attracted his full attention, and he directed his steps toward that voice.

When he reached the place where the voice came from, he discovered a poor and miserable-looking man standing in an empty booth. First he thought to turn on his tracks, then he felt ashamed of himself for having judged the man by his appearance, and with a firm tone he said, 'What are these three words?'

The dervish looked at Amir with astonishment and said to Amir, 'The money first, young man!' It was the first time that Amir had to face such a man. He was caught in a dilemma, as the money he had was the only coin he possessed, but the voice and the words of the dervish inspired him and gave him a feeling of confidence. He sensed that someone close to him was talking, and without further hesitation he handed him the only coin he had. The dervish took him aside and whispered in his ear, 'You see, these people are crazy; they didn't buy the *Golden Words*,' and then with an honest voice he whispered again in his ear, 'My son, why are you buying these words?' Then he continued, 'Are you sure you want to buy words and not merchandise?'

Amir was confused, but a warm feeling filled his suffering heart. Then he remembered his father's words and responded, 'Words are better than money.'

His answer pleased the dervish, and he said to him, 'Listen, and do not give these words to anyone who does not deserve them.' Then he continued, 'the first word is:

If someone is in love with a woman, do not try to change his mind, since for him that woman is always the best and the most beautiful woman on earth.

The second word is:

Be loyal to, and honest with your employer.

The third word is:

Never refuse an invitation to a meal.'

'That's it?' asked the orphaned son.

'Yes, that's what you get for your money,' replied the poor man.

Amir did not dispute the poor man's argument, but he knew that from now on, he was facing the world without a penny. He was desperate, and, to add to his plight, someone reminded him at every corner that his father had owed them money. But deep in his heart he felt that somehow his destiny would lead him in the right direction. He recalled that one day he had heard his father's friend saying that the best decisions he had made in his life were when he had no choice.

Amir didn't have any idea what to do or where to go. Evidently he had no choice. He only knew that he could not stay in the town where he was born, where he could not use the education he had received. Destitute as he was, he decided to let his father's horse lead him, so he would not have to make any choice. *After all, not every*

42

choice that we make is the right one, he murmured. Before he left the town, he visited his father's friends and then went home. Amir took some clothes and some items he wanted to have with him, then he went to the buyer of the house who had been nice to his father, gave him the key of the house, and made his farewells. The new landlord tried to convince him to stay as long as he wanted in the house, but Amir didn't want to change his mind. He departed from his town, leaving behind the good and the sad memories, taking with him only the most necessary belongings for the trip. The new landlord was disappointed, as the young man captivated him, and he thought that he could be a good match for his smart and lovely daughter. Amir had to cross almost an entire desert with his father's horse. As soon as the land changed to desert the horse's step became heavier, as the horse was tired. Silence replaced the tumult of the town. During the day the sun's rays burned Amir's neck, but he kept moving east, hoping to reach any large town or city. He had never experienced the desert heat, which soon gave way to the cold and the darkness of night. But he felt safe and secure, as he did not encounter any trace of a human being. He felt that the desert was alive and that a sort of intelligence was watching over him. For the first time he grasped the connection between himself and the earth.

After a few days and a few nights of riding, and while stopping to quench the horse's thirst, Amir suddenly

looked around him and found himself in a dark and
secluded valley. He unloaded the horse and let it free.
The horse stretched out its body, but it didn't go away as
Amir had assumed. As he was very tired from this long
trip, he murmured, 'We can sleep here; no one can bother
us, and in the morning we can continue our journey
toward the next destination.' The horse seemed to listen
to him. Many thoughts passed through Amir's mind.
Since he had left his house, he hadn't thought about his
mother or about his father. He was absorbed by the
emptiness of the desert and by the darkness of the sky.
He had never had a chance to see such a sky full of stars,
and after a good night's sleep he was awakened by the
noise of his horse, which was running back and forth in
the open valley in bright sunshine. Amir remembered
that he didn't have any more water for the rest of the trip.
While he was trying to reach the next town, both Amir
and the horse were very thirsty. The hunger was not as
terrible as he thought. Far away on the horizon a caravan
of camels was slowly moving toward him, but he
couldn't figure out the distance, as the sun and the sand
were gleaming like a mirror. Amir was dirty and looked
like a beggar. He still had a long way to go. He couldn't
go any further, as the food supply that he had taken with
him had dwindled. He had learned from his father's trips
what kind of vegetation he could eat in the desert, if he
could find it.

44

After almost a month of riding and walking, Amir's strength was decreasing every step of the way, and one evening, as he couldn't see anything anymore in the dark, he fell asleep next to a palm tree. In the morning the people of that large town found him unconscious with his horse standing next to him. As they sprinkled water on him, Amir opened his eyes and saw a crowd gathered around him, and someone was bending over him. Amir thought he was surrounded by thieves and, as he tried to stand up, a lady said to him in a gentle voice, 'Sir, don't be afraid, we are trying to help you', and she gave him some water from her jug. Only then did Amir realize that all the people were assembled around a well and praying. When Amir asked the reason for this gathering, he learned that a giant man was in the well, not letting anyone take water. The king of their city had promised a reward for the one who would free the well. Several strong young men had tried to descend into the well but had not succeeded in obtaining even a drop of water. The population was desperate without water, and they were prepared to take any action that might free the water. When Amir heard this, he decided to try his luck, as he had nothing to lose anymore, but could maybe win a reward.

The people were kind to him, but an old lady said to him, 'It is a pity for a nice young man like you to die.'

He replied, 'My lady, someone has to do it.'

A woman who was listening to him said, 'But young man, out of all the men who tried before you to free the well no one has returned alive. They all lost their lives in the well.'

Amir answered with determination, 'I have to free the water!' and he went into the well, unarmed and without a shirt. When he reached half the depth of the well he saw a recess in the side of the wall like a large room. From this room a giant man appeared holding an ugly woman by one hand and, with the other, pulling the rope Amir was holding on to toward the recess.

The giant man laughed and said, 'Young man, do you want to get water?'

Amir was impressed by the size of the giant man, but he didn't lose his calm or his courage, and with a firm voice he replied, 'I am here to get water, no matter what.'

The giant, confident of his strength, smiled nicely and said, 'I like your tenacity and courage, and I will gladly let you get the water you desire, but not before you answer my simple question first.'

Amir was relieved at the giant's words and said, 'What is your question, Sir?'

The giant smiled again and said, 'Do you see this young lady? Tell me, how do you find her?'

Amir remembered the first word of the three words he had bought with his last ten dinars, ***If someone is in love with a woman, for him this woman is always the best and most beautiful woman on earth,*** and he said to the giant, 'Your lady is lovely. She's so beautiful that, if you were not so strong, I would try to take her away from you.' The giant was extremely pleased with the young man's response; he told him that he could have as much water as he wanted from the well. Now the well was free, and everyone in town could get water again.

In his palace, the king heard about the feat of the young stranger, so he asked to see him. The entire population of the town brought the hero to the king so he might receive his reward. Amir met with the king, and after a short conversation the king found him to be well-educated, well-behaved and smart. He was so impressed by his knowledge that after having given him his reward, he offered the young man a position in his palace. The young man accepted the proposal.

Amir was such a clever and good-looking man that, after a few weeks in his new job, everyone liked him. The king sought his advice, and the queen soon found him very attractive. Many times she used minor excuses to see him, but Amir was very careful not to arouse any negative feelings in the palace. He avoided looking in the eyes of any woman in the king's harem, but her majesty the queen was eager to run into him any time she could.

Amir tried to avoid her, but the queen, who was not busy and had a lot of free time, slowly fell in love with him. Whenever she saw him, she tried to stop and talk to him. One day, she called Amir to her quarters.

When Amir entered her chamber, she unexpectedly embraced him, held him for a while, and said, 'Kiss me!' The charming young man remembered the second word however, ***Be loyal to, and honest with your employer,*** and he refused to give in to her demand. He pushed her away with his arms and freed himself from her embrace. The queen was furious and threatened that if he would not kiss her, she would scream for help and would also accuse him of having tried to force her. When she tried to embrace him again, Amir pushed her aside. She was fuming. The young man was all confused, but he didn't forget for a moment that he had just pushed a queen and a powerful lady. He didn't flee, but stood firm and apologized for his behavior. His conduct seemed to invite the queen for another attempt, but she soon realized that the young man was very smart and aware of his situation. She thought of using the most powerful threat. In her mind she had no choice but to scream, hoping that Amir would finally give up his resistance. After a few attempts she finally cried out loud and alerted the court guards, who came to her aid and apprehended the poor stranger.

The minister, who was jealous of Amir and was not happy that the king hadn't asked for his advice when he had offered Amir the job, found this incident to be a great opportunity to get rid of this young man. When the news about this incident had reached the king's quarters, the king called for the minister, who responded eagerly and immediately. The king asked the minister for advice - how could he punish the young man without attracting the attention of the townspeople? He did not forget that he was after all the one who had freed the well, and he knew that this young hero was popular. Amir was well known to everyone. The minister was thrilled that the king sought his advice, as since Amir had been in the palace he had never consulted him. Amir with all his knowledge was a great threat to the minister. Now the occasion presented itself to put things in order once and for all. He would be able to avenge himself. He came up with a malicious execution plan that he had hastily fabricated for the young man. He told the king that he would cautiously arrange for the young man's disappearance without divulging any detail. The king was embarrassed by this incident, as he was very disturbed about his own poor judgment. He kept repeating that he could not believe that this man, whom he had considered a gentleman, could do something so disloyal and unethical. He couldn't forgive himself for having taken the young man into his confidence and having considered him like his son.

While the king was confused, the minister rushed to coordinate his plan with a man who owned a bakery. He would send Amir to the bakery to ask if the king's bread order was ready; this would be the signal for the baker to identify him and then kill the young man.

The next day, the minister asked Amir if he would like to pick up the king's bread at the bakery. The young hero faithfully and innocently accepted this errand.

To make sure that Amir would convey the message, the minister told him, 'Ask the baker if the king's bread is ready.' Amir accepted and peacefully walked through the town towards the bakery. He walked from street to street to reach his destination and in the middle of the town he came across a group of people gathered together for breakfast. As he greeted them and wished them a pleasant meal, the townspeople returned his greeting and asked him if he would care to join them for breakfast. Amir recalled the third word that he had bought, *Never refuse an invitation to a meal.* So the young man politely accepted the invitation and sat down to eat with them. The people were happy to have Amir as a guest, and they enjoyed his presence. They had a nice conversation with him. All of them remembered that Amir was the one who had freed the well. It was an honor to share a meal with a hero. Everyone wanted to chat with this nice stranger. Luckily it took them a long time to finish the excellent meal. Amir enjoyed the food and

the company. Since his arrival in this town he had never had any contact with anyone. For him this was a great opportunity. While enjoying the conversation, he forgot that he still had to go to the bakery to look for the king's bread.

Meanwhile, and in Amir's absence, the minister grew impatient. Several hours went by, and he was curious to know if the mission had been accomplished. He called his own son and told him to go to the bakery and ask if the king's bread order was ready, so that he could confirm Amir's death to the king. The minister's son went to check for his father. The baker too was impatient. When the minister's son asked if the king's bread was ready, he was not aware of his father's scheme, nor was the baker aware of the minister's intrigue. The baker didn't know what the young man looked like. When the minister's son appeared, the baker grabbed him and threw him into the oven.

Time went by. After his breakfast, Amir courteously thanked the people for their invitation and continued on his way to the baker. He walked slowly and nonchalantly from street to street enjoying the passers-by, as it was the first time since his arrival in this area that he had a chance to walk through town. After a while, and as commanded by the minister, he finally reached his destination. As soon as he reached the bakery, he asked the baker politely for the king's bread. The baker, who was proud

of himself and believed that he had performed the minister's request in return for a reward, answered him, 'Tell the minister that his order had been executed, and that the *bread* in question was burned to the ground.' The young man, unaware of the conspiracy, calmly returned to the palace to convey the strange message to the minister. When the latter saw the young man walking back to his office, he sensed that something had gone wrong. Amir innocently returned to his former job. The minister was trembling as he realized the failure of his own plan. He became very nervous, so he went to the king to inform him of the mishap.

The king, who had never quite believed his queen, called Amir to his chamber, and asked him to relate the story of his life. The honest hero obliged and began. He calmly told about his dedicated mother and father. The king listened attentively and noted with admiration his language and his peaceful state of mind. Amir told him about the three words with special emphasis. The king repeated to himself the second word, ***Be loyal to, and honest with your employer.*** The king felt greatly relieved, as he realized that he had been right in his judgment. He was now totally convinced that the young man was innocent, and he felt sorry for him. He called the queen and confronted her. She finally admitted her wrongdoing. The king exiled her and the unfair minister. He said to the young Amir, 'I believe your story, and I am sorry for the misconduct of my queen and for the

52

minister's intrigue. Your parents were the best parents a human being could have, and you should be proud of them. For the injustice caused to you I will be pleased to keep you in the palace as long as you desire, and later I will consider other new tasks for you'. Eventually Amir pleased the king so much that he decided to give him his only daughter and to appoint him as his successor to the throne. The words had truly been *Golden Words* for the young man."

Once again, Saad the storyteller had captivated his audience with an unusual story, with a moral message, and with a superb performance. The caliph stood up, and so did all the dignitaries, to give the Jewish storyteller a standing ovation. Then the caliph thanked Saad for accepting his invitation. After a while he retreated to his quarters and called for Saad to join him there. The caliph chatted with Saad and enjoyed his company. Then he wished him a safe trip back to Jerusalem.

A few weeks later, and despite the pleasure he had experienced listening to Saad's lovely story, Harun Al-Rashid plunged again into distress and pain, and no one was able to relieve him from his memories. He felt a burning flame in his chest, which was about to consume him. Sometimes he sensed that he had to keep this fire alive to be worthy of his wife's love.

Chapter 4

Seeking Relief

Many months had passed since the pleasant evening with Saad the storyteller. The caliph woke up one day with his heart aching. No one knew what to do to relieve him from the sorrow he was experiencing. His state of mind was at its lowest, and even his daughter couldn't lift his spirits. He was blaming himself, as he could not comprehend how, with all his power and his fortune, he had not managed to save his wife's life. Looking up to the ceiling, as though in deep thought, he remembered that in the beginning Zaafer Lebranki had strongly objected to the choice of Farha, the day he first met her, because she came from a well to do but not noble family. That day, Zaafer Lebranki had put his life at risk when he said, "My lord, you cannot marry a lady without a noble background."

But at that time the king had responded angrily and said, "So you make her a princess and I will make her my queen!" Zaafer Lebranki had no other choice but to obey his master, as did his father before him. It was

indeed a hard task for Zaafer to design a plan that would transform this simple woman into a rich princess. It had cost a fortune for the treasury to create the appearance of a noble genealogy for the young girl.

Zaafer never forgot that day, when the king entrusted him with this tedious and unrewarding task. The caliph, on one hand, had always considered his wife to be the noblest and wisest of all the princesses that had been presented to him, but on the other hand he knew full well that Farha had only become a princess due to his power and his position. When he made his choice of Farha, he had trusted his feelings. This is why he had rejected all the princesses who had been introduced to him by Zaafer. He now believed silently that the fact of Zaafer Lebranki's objection to choosing Farha had turned his great happiness into pain, although he had no factual reason for his suggestion. Since then he had mistrusted Zaafer.

General Omar knew the entire story of Farha's background, but as a man of trust and as a soldier he preferred to keep everything to himself and not to share this confidence with anyone. He had never shown any objection to the king's choice unless it was a matter of security. His attitude earned him the king's esteem. The king was happy that the general, for whom he had a lot of respect, understood his feelings, but the general had another agenda and other interests in mind. He never

56

revealed to anyone but the king that he was of pure Arabian origin and not of Persian origin like Zaafer Lebranki or the king. This fact never bothered the king, especially after the great victory that General Omar won for him.

At that time, Khayet was almost grown-up. She was tall and surpassed her mother in both beauty and intelligence. When she saw her father deeply saddened that morning, she said, "Father, shortly before passing away, my mother told me how you met her for the first time. She also told me that she actually did not come from a noble family."

When the caliph heard this, he put his hand on her mouth and made her promise never to talk again about this with anyone in the world. Of course, Khayet was smart, and she smiled the same way her mother used to. Harun Al-Rashid was surprised at the resemblance Khayet had to Farha. For a moment, it seemed to him that he was looking into his wife's eyes. It was like a message that he received. He recalled that before the time when he discovered his wife, he liked to mingle with the people, disguised as a common man. This thought gave him the idea of disguising himself again and of mingling with his people. Suddenly, the king smiled for the first time to his daughter Khayet and said, "My dear daughter, my heart is filled with bitterness. I would like to disguise myself and wander outside the

palace for a while without telling anyone. Can you keep this secret?"

Khayet, noticing that his eyes had lit up and that life was coming back into her father, seized the opportunity and answered, "My dear father, you know how much I love you, and how much I love my mother. If you go outside, the sun will shine again in your heart and I will be very happy." Khayet smiled and continued, "Father, please go out and enjoy the day, you can count on me to keep this secret."

The caliph was moved by her kind words and for the first time, he felt that his heart was healing. Then, with a kind smile, he told her, "I will be back before the sun sets." Khayet was very happy to see her father regain life, as she could conclude from his attitude and behavior.

He found the old disguise that had served him years ago and managed to leave the palace unnoticed. He had taken enough money with him to be ready for any event. As soon as he turned into the first side street of the town, he ran into a peasant on a horse. He stopped him and asked, "Sir, excuse me please, are you from this area?"

The peasant, with an innocent attitude, smiled and said, "I wish I was from this neighborhood that you see in front of you."

The king looked in the direction indicated by the passer-by and said, "If this is your wish, I may be the

right person. How much do you need to fulfill your wish?"

The peasant looked at him with an astonished face and said, "If I had just one hundred dinars, I would be able to move to that nice quiet area."

The king, who wanted to know more about this peasant, asked him, "How much do you earn in one month?"

The peasant, who had sensed from his words that he was dealing with an honest person, answered with a loud laugh, "Less than ten dinars."

The caliph reached into his pocket and pulled out three gold coins of one hundred dinars each. He handed the coins to the peasant and said, "For how long will these three coins keep you going?"

The peasant smiled like a child and said, "Almost three years, Sir."

The peasant had never seen such big gold coins, and he responded nimbly and fearfully, "Sir, I think that you are mistaking me for someone else, and before answering your generous offer, please understand that I am a common man and all my possessions are not worth one coin of yours. If the king's guards catch me with such a sum of money, they will put me in their dark jail."

The caliph smiled happily for recognizing such an honest man and said, "No, no, Sir, I would like you to give me your horse and your cape for these three coins; they are worth it." The peasant didn't know how to react to such an offer. Then he thought quietly, three hundred dinars could buy him a new house, a better horse than the one he had, and the last coin would be enough money to put on the side. But he was so good that he was scared to fall into a security trap. The king with his disguise could well be a foreign spy who wanted to recruit him for who knows what purpose or mission. He knew that his horse was not worth even one tenth of the golden coin. The peasant tried to guess whether the buyer was not a thief; then he said to himself, *Judging by his words and his appearance, he is probably a nobleman*, although his disguise did not allow the peasant to identify him. He was attracted by such a generous sum of money. The peasant looked left and right and up and down the street, to see if anybody was watching from a window, and when he saw that the street was empty, he quickly dismounted from his horse, took off his cape, handed it to the caliph, took the three gold coins, and said, "Be careful, the caliph's guards are everywhere in town", thinking that this man was a stranger. From the peasant's advice, Harun Al-Rashid understood that the people feared his guards. Such information was of great value to the king, and he was happy for having engaged in this adventure. Many years had passed since he had gone out

of the palace. He was breathing once again the fresh air of his country. He was also pleased that this encounter didn't reveal his identity. He mounted the peasant's horse and carefully rode through the streets of the town, observing his subjects. He enjoyed the freedom of horseback-riding without anyone telling him what to do. Then, turning the reins, he guided the horse into a parallel street that seemed empty and calm; only one dog was there. While he thought he was entering a busy street, he was in fact turning into a deserted one. He looked left and right, and at the edge of the town something attracted his attention. He was feeling the cold air of the morning and as he was about to enter another street he saw something from afar that looked like a monument surrounded by benches. Then he saw the shadow of a person. The caliph waited for a moment for a passer-by to come along. He stopped him politely and asked, "Sir, what is that round structure there?"

The man smiled, and then he said, "You are not from this area?" The caliph made a gesture with his head meaning no, then the passer-by continued, "Thank our king! He built the big well for the people."

Al-Rashid thanked him and, in order not to appear suspicious, said, "Let's have a drink of water on the caliph's account." The passer-by went on his way, and the caliph continued towards the new well. Slowly, Al-Rashid regained his confidence and hope and directed his

horse towards the well. The horse advanced at a slow pace on the street that was paved with slippery stones. On both sides of the street and through the shades of the windows, many women's eyes could be seen following the stranger's path. The king noticed that someone was looking at him. When he reached the place of the well, there were other women washing their belongings at the small pond built for them that lay next to the well. From there it was difficult to recognize the approaching king.

Nearby, there were a few benches built of stone. There he encountered a well-dressed lady sitting on one of the benches. Since the passing of his wife, Harun Al-Rashid could not remember having been interested in any woman. From the moment he saw her, he was confident that this lady would fill the big void left by the passing of his wife. He tried to find nice words with which to approach her, but all his knowledge and his eloquence disappeared. He kept his hope and faith that this was the woman he was waiting for. She was elegantly dressed, and her look gave her the appearance of a noble woman. Her face was white in contrast with her deep dark eyes. She was holding something in her hand and was not looking at the king at all, but when she turned her head toward the well her eyes met with the king's eyes. The king felt a very pleasant sensation. He kept turning with his horse in order to see her again and again. The lady didn't react; her head was facing the

opposite direction. The king became eager to see her eyes again.

He dismounted his horse and walked slowly toward her. Again, as he looked at her, he sensed a sweet energy coming from a deep source, capturing his whole being. He could see the stillness of the night in her black eyes. Moved as he was, he knew that he was facing someone very strong, with a distinct destiny. He looked at her once more, so as to enjoy the sensation he was experiencing. When she saw that someone was approaching, she looked directly in his eyes. This time the king was almost trembling at the expression in her eyes, and while advancing closer and closer he said, "My dear lady, you may not believe me, but since I saw you, your eyes have captured my heart." Then he paused and went on, "My heart is burning with an unknown fire."

The lady looked into his eyes. She saw his white and noble face and said, "Sir, your horse and your clothes are those of a simple farmer, but your language and your attitude are those of a noble man, if not a king."

The caliph was deeply moved by her astuteness, and he responded, "My lady, I am not a farmer, as you said, but if you dare believe me, I will make of you the best woman on earth."

She looked at him again. This time she was fully confident in her heart that she was dealing with an honest person, and with a reassuring tone she said, "Sir, I was

the best woman on earth for my beloved husband. Unfortunately the last epidemic took him from me." From the look of her eyes, the king could see the sorrow that resembled the feelings he had been having since his wife had passed away. Soraya looked at him and continued, "Sir, I believe you, as you look like a decent man, and especially, as the ring on your finger is not a common one."

The caliph was taken by her sharp observation. He was impatient to respond, and said, "My lady, I can no longer wait. What you are saying is adding fire in my heart; I will no longer let you waste your dear time. As you said, I am not a common man. If you are not already engaged again, I dare ask you to marry me."

The widow started to worry. This time she was facing a real challenger. Until now she had succeeded in discouraging all her admirers. She felt that this time the man represented a true danger to her and to her only son. With a soft and sad voice she responded, "I was married to my cousin, and before he died I vowed to him not to marry another man after him. As for your question, I am not engaged to anyone." Then she added, "Do you understand what I mean? If you are a man of honor, you will respect my vow and my decision."

Al-Rashid sighed with pain, as he too had made a vow. One could see the sadness in his eyes. The widow saw that this gentleman was also suffering from

something unknown to her. Then, with a thoughtful gesture, she said, "I hope I didn't unintentionally insult you."

The kind consideration that this lady was showing had not escaped the king's attention. He increasingly felt his heart filled with a burning love that no one could see. Deep within himself he understood and wanted to respect her vow, but somehow her decision gave him further reason to insist on asking for her hand. Her answer strengthened his belief that this lady was the most appropriate for him. He wanted her more than before, and he knew that this kind of woman would be well received by the entourage of his palace. He kept repeating to himself, *A woman who did not bow to my charm, a woman who understood my pain, and a woman who could be a good stepmother for my daughter Khayet.* " These arguments strengthened his resolve to have her as the next queen. Then, with the tone of a man of power, and with a firm gesture, he turned toward her, so that he could again face her eyes, and said, "My lady, no one in the entire empire can understand your suffering and your pain like this humble man. I myself also made a vow to my deceased wife not to get married again, but I believe that there is a reason why destiny brought us both here to this place. We are the only ones who can relieve the pain in each other's heart. Please listen to me for a moment and let your heart decide. I will marry you with all the honor you deserve, and I will leave the type

of ceremony to your discretion, and of course to my account. Furthermore, I will bring the Ten Elders of the Holy Koran to absolve you and myself from our vows." As she was preparing to answer him, Al-Rashid spoke first. He knew from her look that her answer would be negative. To prevent her from hastily saying something he would not like to hear, he said in a majestic voice, "Will you please stop thinking? You are sitting on my bench and drinking my water."

The widow countered emphatically, "Pardon me, how dare you make such an accusation? The well and the benches were built and donated by our generous king," and she indicated with her finger a marble plate on which there was written, "Built by His Majesty Caliph Harun Al-Rashid for his people." The caliph was pleased with her response. He started laughing so much that she felt uncomfortable, and she countered with another outburst, "Do you see now that I am not sitting on your bench?"

The caliph felt uneasy for having brought up such a trivial matter. He apologized by saying, "My lady, I am sorry for having been ungraceful. Of course, you can sit on the bench as long as you like. It is a privilege given to you by your king."

To show him that she was well informed and that she had a good relationship with the palace people, the widow said, "I love my king, and I will do anything for him."

The caliph was delighted to hear these words. Now, he thought that all he had to do was to tell her that he was the caliph of Baghdad and the king of Persia, and everything would be in place. He smiled graciously and said, "My lady, I thank you for your kind words. I too will do anything for you. To begin, here is my royal ring; I give it to you as a small token. Your dowry will of course be much larger than any man can give." In that region there was a custom that the man give a wedding gift to his bride. He continued, "You can now open your heart to me. I am your king; I am Harun Al-Rashid in person, and if you don't believe me, here is my seal."

The widow, using a sweet voice so as not to irritate him, bowed and responded, "My king, the powerful one and the great one of all kings, from your ring I recognized you, but I didn't dare express my feelings, as I was not sure, with all the torments and the harassment I am enduring. With all respect to Your Majesty, I am afraid of every man." She wiped her eyes, as was usual at that time when an honorable man spoke to a lady, and continued, "What an honor to see you in person without any formality. Since my husband died, I haven't encountered any decent man. I hope you will understand my feelings towards men."

The caliph said in a conciliatory voice, full of joy, "I understand your repugnance. You don't have to suffer

anymore; you will be under royal protection. Just say yes, and all your prayers will be answered."

The widow realized that the caliph was insisting, and she felt that she had to tell him the truth without delay. With a gentle but firm voice she said, "My king, excuse my sharp response to you. I wish I had known before that you were my dear king, whom my heart and my son's heart were longing to meet, and to tell you how much we understand your pain and your suffering. We knew about the passing of your dear and beloved wife, Queen Farha. Please forgive me for having spoken to you with a harsh voice." The heart of the king softened and melted from her charm and her sweetness. He became vulnerable, as he never displayed his suffering to anyone except his daughter and Zaafer Lebranki, his closest friend. Now he was prepared to conquer her without hurting her feelings, especially since she had unveiled her feminine charm. He considered various approaches. He was also confused, but the widow wanted to be clear and, before the king had time to formulate his response, she continued, "My king, my love for you is more than my love for my husband," as she said these words, the king was completely overwhelmed and wanted to respond, but she took the initiative again and continued, "but it is a different kind of love. I am willing to be your sister if you accept me in your family." He nodded to show understanding, and then she continued, "I know the

68

suffering you endured for your wife. My sister and I will serve you better than anyone."

The king was once again confused. He thought that her response was positive, but not clear. If she made reference to her sister, she probably wanted to move into the palace with her sister. He answered very softly, "My dear lady, your sister is welcome; we can give her an apartment in the palace so she won't be far from you. We will do our best to accommodate all her needs."

When she saw that her words were misinterpreted, she spoke with a firm voice without losing either her charm or her respect for the king, and said, "I loved my husband very much, and before he died I promised to him and to Allah not to get married again." When she finished talking, the caliph could not comprehend how a woman like this could refuse the hand of a king. After all, she was only a woman, and according to Muslim law women had less value than men. He was furious, as he knew that he couldn't bear any new affliction. He mounted his horse, and without saying a word, he turned in the direction of the palace to see his closest friend and adviser Zaafer Lebranki. As she saw that he was about to leave, she said, "My king, I hope you understand, and I believe you know my father." When the king heard her say this, he turned around and saluted her. He then continued on his way.

The king quickened the step of his horse to show a kind of broken feeling. The widow noticed his anger and said to herself, *God protect me from this kind of anger.*

Chapter 5

The Judgment

Meanwhile, the caliph was far away and had disappeared over the horizon. The widow too left the well and went toward her house. She cried in pain, her cheeks streaming with tears. She was charming, and every passer-by turned his head to look at her. As she approached her street a young and very handsome man saw her and told her politely and with dignity, "My lady, is there anything I can do for you?"

The lady, without even thinking for a moment, answered, "Oh yes, you can do something; go and appease your king!" The poor young man looked at her and thought that the lady must be suffering from something. He waved his hand and continued on his way.

The caliph was still in his disguise when he reached the palace. He entered the same way as he had left, and no one saw him. As soon as he reached his quarters, he called for Zaafer Lebranki to come and see him immediately. When the *wazir* received the message, he didn't know what had happened to the caliph, but the

tone of the messenger alarmed him. He went quickly and took his assistant with him in case he should need him. He entered the caliph's room, leaving his assistant behind the door. When the caliph saw Zaafer Lebranki, he addressed him with these words, "Zaafer Lebranki, are you still my adviser and my closest friend? Your father served this dynasty before I was born."

Zaafer Lebranki's concern grew. He responded, "Just tell me what happened to you and why you are dressed like this?"

The caliph was no longer calm and replied, "My dear Zaafer Lebranki, you know how much I value your advice and your service."

Zaafer Lebranki's impatience grew, as he thought that the caliph may have been attacked and stripped by a gang of thieves. He said, "If you tell me who did that to you, I will have his head taken off."

The caliph nervously responded, "My dear friend, tell me what to do with this lady?"

Zaafer Lebranki was stunned to see the caliph in such a terrible state, and spoke, "What happened to you, my king?"

The caliph said with an alarming tone, "She wants to kill me!"

Zaafer Lebranki was in shock, as he didn't know anything about the caliph's secret excursion. He answered, "My king, where was the guard?" Then he called the chief guard to him. When he arrived, Zaafer Lebranki inquired anxiously, "Where was all our security?"

The caliph, realizing that he had created confusion, quickly interrupted Zaafer Lebranki and in a calmer tone said, "Send back the guard and let me tell you the entire story."

Zaafer Lebranki sent the guard away, closed the door behind him, stood in front of the caliph, and said, "My king, I am sorry! I will punish the head of my security for this incident." The king gave permission to Zaafer Lebranki to sit down and started recounting his adventure. When he had finished talking, Zaafer Lebranki first took the attitude of a man who can solve every problem and said in an assuring tone, "My king, your problem is a tiny matter to me. Go see your daughter and relax, and tomorrow I will make sure that the widow comes to your palace to see you on her knees." Zaafer Lebranki took a few notes and as soon as the caliph left for his daughter's room, he assembled his security men and gave them all the instructions necessary. Then he ordered the head of security and told him, "Arrange a dispute between the widow's son and a few youths and make sure that we have enough witnesses

to say that the widow's son insulted the caliph. The guards of course will be there too, to arrest him. Then we will put him in a dark cell in the jail of our palace. Once the news reaches his mother - and make sure that she hears the news - she will come to the palace to see the caliph. Then it will be up to the caliph to decide." Zaafer Lebranki's plan seemed to satisfy the security men. The caliph arrived at his daughter's quarters with a happier face. Meanwhile, Zaafer Lebranki made all the necessary arrangements for his mission to succeed.

The next day, before noon, the news circulated in the widow's neighborhood, that her son had been arrested by the guards on the pretext that he had insulted the caliph and his secretary Zaafer Lebranki. Her neighbor came to tell her that her son was not only jailed, but that he had been chained and badly beaten, and that his face was beyond recognition. He added that he had received this information from a friend who worked in the palace jail.

The poor widow understood that Zaafer Lebranki had created a fabrication and that they purposely committed an injustice against her son in order to get to her. She put on her best dress and went directly to see the caliph in his palace. She was determined not to give in to his capricious love and was prepared to use strong words and speak out resolutely. This time the widow was desperate, adamant to fight back and not to succumb to the caliph's love. That day she looked more beautiful

74

THE KING AND THE WIDOW

than on any other day. She murmured to herself, *Oh, my poor child, I will get you out, no matter what.* She wiped her eyes and said, *My dear child, they committed a crime against you. I will not rest until justice is done, for the love of your father, my dear husband.* Her heart beat faster as she approached the palace, but her attitude impressed every passer-by. Meanwhile, many residents of Baghdad who had witnessed the fate of her son had spread her story so fast that the local population was inflamed. When she reached the palace, a huge crowd was already assembled in front of the gate. They protested the imprisonment of her son, but she was not sure if this was the real reason. She did not want to appear associated with the crowd, for fear of being drawn into political turmoil, which she had always tried to avoid, on her late father's advice. From his window, the caliph followed her steps. The crowd didn't impress him at all, as he was used to seeing groups of the population protesting for one reason or another. His main thought was that he was going to see the widow in his palace. He was full of himself and believed that when she saw him dressed in his royal robes, she would not be able to resist his charm any longer, and she would certainly change her mind.

As she advanced, step by step, the king was already planning out his royal wedding with the widow. He was sure that he would convince Zaafer Lebranki with his plan. His daughter was his main concern, as he didn't

know how she would receive the news. He had yet to convince her, but he preferred to leave this thinking for another time. He was greatly relieved by this last development. He would tell his daughter soon after seeing the widow. His eyes lighted up like a child's eyes; his whole being was filled with joy; but just before entering his reception room, he suddenly felt sad. He did not know the reason for this sudden change of mood. As he walked slowly to see the widow, the face of his deceased wife appeared in his mind; he didn't know if it was real or if he was experiencing a dream. This thought was about to disturb his day. When he entered the hall, Zaafer Lebranki and the widow were just arriving. Seeing Zaafer Lebranki with the widow bothered him, but he didn't show it. He smiled, to appear majestic. At the very moment his eyes met the widow's eyes, he smiled again, but the widow returned a serious and severe look. She addressed him while staring into his eyes and said, "My king, do not think for a moment that you will succeed because you hold power."

The caliph, who didn't expect such an outburst from her, was shocked. He remained calm, so as not to appear vulgar. His aim was to capture her heart, not to arouse her defensive strength. The caliph answered with an earnest but kind face, "My lady, what made you so upset?" and he continued, "What reason brought you here?"

"What do you take me for, my king?"

As Zaafer Lebranki hadn't had time to apprise the king of her son, the king answered her, "I consider you a most beautiful and noble lady."

"That's all that you have to say, my king?" But she continued, "You are a man of honor and dignity. Judge me in an open court and in front of the public, and I will accept any sentence."

The caliph felt that she had gone too far, daring to insult him in front of his secretary and the guard, but he remained calm. Zaafer Lebranki took him aside for a moment, to tell him about her son. Then, the king came back and said to her, "As you wish, my lady. I will hold an open court in three months' time, and your son's case will be decided by the public." A smile flitted across his face, then he added, "Your wish is granted, my lady."

The widow was confused, and her face flushed with embarrassment. Then she thought of her poor son and took a deep breath. When she heard that the caliph would hold a public court within three months, she thought that it would be better not to delay the judgment for that long, for the sake of her son. She preferred to let the caliph judge her immediately, to spare her son another three months of suffering. She responded, this time with a smile and a gentle voice, "My king, the longer I see you, the more I realize that I misjudged you, and if you allow me to change my mind...."

As he heard these words, he interjected, "My lady, I knew from the beginning that you were the right lady for me, and I apologize for any inconvenience caused to you by my security people. I knew that you would change your mind. Can a lady like you find a better position than that of a queen?"

The widow was again disappointed, and as she didn't want to give the king false hopes, she said, "That is not what I meant. I wanted to say that I'd rather be judged by you than by a public court. I trust your judgment."

The caliph interrupted her, "Ah ha, you thought of everything!"

Then he apologized for not letting her finish her sentence, and she continued, "My king, you just have to name the price for the release of my son. If I am not able to pay it, I will marry you in a religious ceremony."

The caliph was happy to hear this proposal. He first conferred with Zaafer Lebranki, then again with an ironic and gentle smile he said, "My dear lady, the price for your son's release is a tiny matter. I am prepared to forget his insult; just bring me one thousand and one young female camels, all of them one year of age and in every existing color, and I will release your son from jail, and the case will be closed."

78

Chapter 6

The Old Man

When the widow heard this, she was relieved that the sentence was a material one, but her heart sank when she realized the extent of the caliph's demand. She thanked the caliph and his secretary and left the palace with tears in her eyes. The caliph knew exactly that such a number of camels did not exist in the whole region and that she would soon be discouraged and come back for the wedding. As soon as the palace ladies and the servants heard of the caliph's judgment, they discreetly showed a great deal of compassion for the widow. Everyone discussed Zaafer Lebranki's advice. The widow's tears flowed without stopping. She prayed to God to show her where she could find such a huge number of yearling camels. She had no idea where she should start to look. As she advanced, her steps became heavier and heavier. She was devastated. Then she went to the place where she had met the caliph. She sat down on the bench, still crying, when she suddenly saw an elderly but strong man sitting on the same bench where she had been sitting the

day before. He looked at her and said, "My dear lady, I do not know the reason for your distress, but do tell me your story. I am sure that I can find a solution." The old man's voice was compassionate and seemed sincere. The widow felt comfortable; she sat down on the bench next to him and told him the entire story. The old man listened with patience, and when she had finished he looked at her and said, "My lady, what you are telling me is a real love story, but first eat something with me, and afterwards I will send you to a village, two days distance from here, and there you will find the answer to the caliph's demand."

After lunch the widow regained her confidence, and a faint smile appeared in her eyes. Then she looked at the old man and said, "Whatever you tell me to do, I will follow without hesitation, as I have a feeling that God sent you to me."

The old man looked at her as though he were looking at his own child and told her, "My lady, how can a man allow a beautiful woman like you to cry? Please wash your face and listen to me patiently."

The widow thanked him and washed her face at the nearby well. Then she sat again next to him, like a child next to her father, and said, "Go on, I am listening."

The old man began, "I will show the king that, if he is in love with you, he should not have done what he did."

These words coming from an old and serious man comforted the widow and gave her assurance that the old man surely had a solution. She was looking forward to seeing the caliph's reaction, but as she didn't know what the old man had in mind, she stopped short of laughing. The old man continued, "You will go on horseback to Si Bousid El Hallali, who lives, as I told you before lunch, two days from here." As she heard "two days" the poor Soraya figured out that without a horse she would need at least ten days on foot. Her face showed some concern. The old man repeated, "I told you before not to worry; I have the solution for everything." The widow looked at him with an innocent smile. This smile didn't pass unnoticed by the old fox. He too laughed and repeated, "I know it is not easy in this world to trust an unknown man, but please have patience and you will see very clearly in a moment. If you have concerns, I don't blame you; if you couldn't trust your own king, who am I to be trusted? But I am just asking you to listen; afterwards, the choice is yours."

Now the widow seemed reassured by the answer. She apologized to him and said, "I am sorry, please continue. I was just thinking of my son."

The old man, with a kind face, said to her, "I understand your concern, but wait patiently and you will see what happens." He thought for a moment, then he paused to take a deep breath and continued with a serious

and loving voice, "You see the hill far away over there, which is at about half a day's distance? You will come to the Euphrates River, and then you will cross the river and stay on the right bank for about one day. You will see the first village and then continue another half day. Then you will see the village of Si Bousid. Everyone knows him. He is the leader of this great village, and every surrounding village follows him and works for him. Si Bousid is a very rich man. He did a lot of good for his villagers. He doesn't like the caliph very much. He will see your beauty and will not let you go empty-handed."

Again the widow was sad and her face was serious. The old man was kind and patient with her and stopped to let her ponder. Then, after a long while, he smiled gently and said, "Do you feel better now? Can I continue?"

The widow again apologized for changing her face every time he spoke. With a soft voice she said, "Please continue."

The old man smiled again and told her, "If you did not have feelings, I would neither have spoken to you, nor volunteered to help you. I was in the palace, heard the caliph's unjust verdict, and I determined to help you. I was the first to go out of the palace and with my horse I came to this place, knowing that you would pass by."

The widow was again disturbed and interrupted him, "But where is your horse? What were you doing in the palace?" The widow thought that this time she was certainly again the victim of a plot engineered by Zaafer Lebranki.

The old man was eager to know if she would trust him. He sat quietly and continued with the same reassuring tone, "I agree with you, your questions are legitimate ones, you deserve a clear and unequivocal answer." The widow was about to leave, but after listening to him she chose to give him the benefit of the doubt and let him answer the questions. The old man did not show any sign of impatience, he was sitting comfortably on the bench. The widow watched him with admiration; to his merit she trusted him, but did not want to show it. Then the old man said, "My horse is attached to the tree behind the hill. Why was I in the palace? This morning I received a delegation of elders asking me to intervene; somehow they knew about a young boy who was known by many of my friends."

"But you did not intervene for me with the caliph at the palace," interrupted the widow. Then she let him continue to talk, although she was eager to know who these people were, who knew her son. But she abstained from asking; at that moment she preferred to let him talk.

"You are right," said the old man, "I did not intervene because, when someone is in love, it becomes a matter

of prestige and not of reason." Then he looked at her and added, "Did you see the caliph? He seemed to be in pain." He paused and sighed, "It reminded me of the days of his great conquests and of his glory. I noticed the changing mood of the caliph every time I went to the palace. For me it is a question of dignity and honor." The widow didn't understand what he was alluding to. Then he said, "Now you understand what I mean?"

The widow didn't want to insult him, so she said, "Yes, of course." She realized that he was old, but he was still strong. She wondered who this old man was and why he wanted to help her. In his eyes she could see his honesty and goodness. Finally she was relaxed, and he was happy.

Then he continued, "My lady, I hope I have passed the test of confidence and that I may continue my directions about the route you are to take." Then, with a serious tone, he went on, "After you cross the river, I said you have to follow the right river bank and you will find a small village. Do not stop at that village, but continue until you reach a second and larger village. You enter that second village. From afar you will see a large house painted white. The door and the windows are painted blue and green. In any case, the horse knows the village and the house. He will lead you directly to Bousid."

When she heard about the horse, she again interrupted him and said, "Will I have to go alone in the wilderness?"

84

The old man smiled and said, "You will have a horse." The poor widow didn't know how all this had developed, and she thanked him for his generosity and kindness. In fact she was nervous; with all the guidance and the route description, she was wondering how she would succeed in this enormous task without help and without a man with her. She tried to repeat what the old man had just said, but she couldn't remember. When the old man had finished talking, he stood up, turned his face towards a small hill, and waited for a moment. Suddenly a white horse appeared and was walking towards him. Then he lifted his left hand towards the sky, and the horse, which seemed well trained, galloped towards his master. The old man turned to the widow and said, "Here is my horse. He will obey you the same way he obeys me."

The widow was moved by his gesture, but she didn't know how to thank him. In the back of her mind she had felt comfortable, although she could not understand why the old man wanted to help her. She observed him carefully, but couldn't find a sign of any malicious intent, or any wrong gesture, or any hint from the old man's face. She found him decent and straightforward. She decided not to deal with her feelings for the moment; the first priority was to get her son out of the palace prison. In any event, the old man seemed determined to help. She remembered two of her father's sayings. The

first, *No one does something for nothing*, and the second saying, *Take what is given to you*. She agreed with both sayings, but she preferred starting with the second one. Meanwhile the old man had noticed some change in her face. He attributed this change to her son's problem. Then he turned his head again towards the hill, lifted his hand twice, and this time a tall man appeared from behind the hill holding the bridle of a horse in his hand. He walked in their direction. She was not sure if this man was coming to the old man or just walking in their direction by coincidence. While she watched the advancing man, she said to the old man, "I didn't see you in the palace."

He replied, "You could not have seen me; I was behind the door listening to what the caliph was saying." Then he smiled and added, "You recall when he said, 'My dear lady, my demand is simple and of small matter . . . .' Do you believe that his demand was a light one?"

She answered, "Not at all!"

Then he went on, "You recall when you entered the caliph's room, Zaafer Lebranki was on his left side."

"Yes, I had noticed this. Normally, the secretary would have been on his right side, would he not?"

He smiled again in agreement and went on, "Do you believe now that I was there in the palace?"

86

The widow murmured, *He could not have known my story if he had not been there.* Then she said, "I can see that you know more than I thought." On the other hand, she was again questioning his sincerity. She doubted whether he was not an agent of the king, or even worse, an agent of Zaafer Lebranki. The tall man was now at a closer distance to her and he saluted the old man. That sent a cold shiver down her back. At this point, she was persuaded that a conspiracy against her was going on. She played back, without showing any sign of question in her mind, every word that had been said during the short time since she had met the old man. While the tall man was talking with the old man, she was pondering if she should interrupt their conversation. Then she considered, on one hand, if she would not follow his advice and they were real agents of Zaafer Lebranki, they might try to find other ways to get her. On the other hand, she had nothing to lose if she followed the advice of the old man; at least she would not have to blame herself for not having tried. She finally reached a conclusion, to give the old man a chance.

She was interrupted in her deliberations when the old man introduced the tall man to her by saying, "The colonel will be leading your escort, and he will be responsible for the trip and for your safety. He will be joined by ten of the best guards." She liked the word safety but she recalled the day when her father sent her

to her aunt with his guard to watch for her safety. That guard tried to abuse her, but he didn't succeed due to her vigilance. She reasoned that, since she had left the palace, time was very short for Zaafer Lebranki to organize any scheme against her. The colonel was watching her furtively as she was speaking with the old man. He was eager to accompany her. It had been a long time since he had last accompanied the queen. Since then, he had not been offered any similar service for any other lady. At that time he was still in the royal army. He had kept good relations with the old man.

The widow was now eager to undertake this long trip and get it over with. She was hoping that after this trip she would be able to obtain the release of her son who was paying with his suffering for her charm and beauty. Nothing else was on her mind except for her son Rahman. She hoped that he would come out of this ordeal without any damage to his health. She knew very well from her father's saying that the jail in the palace was terrible and that the guards there were very harsh.

Rahman was very handsome and resembled his father; he enjoyed life to the fullest. If he stayed in jail for too long, he might become permanently ill. When his father had died, he was very sad and didn't want to talk to anyone. His mother had to move to Baghdad with him, so that he could make new friends. It was a long time before he regained his normal habits. Rahman loved his

father very much. He had also promised his father not to let anyone marry his mother. The widow did not know about her son's promise to his father.

The colonel was joined by ten guards on horses. They had all been in the war under the colonel's command and had great experience as soldiers. One of them was pulling the colonel's horse behind him. Everything seemed to be going as planned, as in the army. The widow had figured out that the old man had chosen the colonel because he could rely on him for security matters. When all the guards and the colonel were ready to go, the old man gave his final advice to the widow and helped her mount his white horse. Then he said, "God be with you." Then he spoke alone with the colonel, gave him a letter, and waved with his hand.

Chapter 7

The Expedition

After all the thoughts and the doubt, the widow was finally at peace with herself and went happily with the colonel. He was a charming man and seemed to be from a noble family, as he was well educated. The sky was clear and bright, and the sun was burning the widow's white skin. The ten guards rode in military formation. One guard was in front of the colonel; behind him was the widow, and then one guard on each side. At a fair distance from her, two guards were following far behind her, and one guard was following the small caravan's trail. These six guards formed a cross, and the last four guards were riding around the caravan at a distance of a few hundred yards on each side. The colonel had planned the formation the way he used to plan a military movement when he served under General Omar. He didn't want to take any chances; he had given his assurance to the old man that he would lead the widow to his son and return her safely to the palace. After a few hours under the hot sun, the widow realized that she was

in good hands. The guards didn't talk or stop without the colonel's sign of approval.

The colonel entertained the widow by informing her of every small hill and answering her questions. The widow felt comfortable and safe with him. When she asked him at what time he thought they would reach the large river, he showed her the direction with his hand and said, "You see the dunes? Just behind them you will see the river." Then he said, "My name is Rabiya."

The widow didn't want to miss this opportunity, so she answered, "Welcome, my name is Soraya!"

Rabiya replied, "Ahla wa sahla!" (Welcome). He turned his head slightly and smiled. That was the first time that Soraya saw his white teeth. The horses were moving like sea waves. Soraya saw the colonel make some signals to his guards, and the guards slowed down. The guard who was behind them moved suddenly to the front, while the guard in the front approached the colonel and whispered something. The widow didn't understand what they were saying, but she realized that something was going on. The guard in the front and the guard behind left at great speed. Soraya couldn't see where they went. Their horses moved like lightning. Then the colonel spoke with two other guards, and they too left the caravan, heading south. It was a scary moment. The silence of the desert intensified the atmosphere of danger.

The colonel noticed that Soraya was somewhat concerned and even anxious; he apprised her of what was going on, "My lady, my guards have encountered some thieves who wanted to surprise us by hiding behind a small dune. We will show them with whom they are dealing."

In a matter of minutes, the four guards were moving back slowly. One of them made a sign. The colonel smiled and said, "Our guards inflicted heavy damage on them. They will never try again."

Soraya didn't understand this language and said, "What do you mean by heavy damage?"

He answered, "They lost their horses; they thought to leave them behind another dune. One of our guards realized this, went behind the dune, freed the horses and chased them far away. The guard took care of the thieves. He beat them, removed all their loot, and emptied their pockets. This time they let them escape with their lives; next time they will think twice." Soraya was impressed, but she felt sorry for the thieves and asked the colonel whether they could survive without water or food. The colonel responded briefly, "This is the law of the desert. I stayed with you to protect you against any other thief that may have escaped my guards' eyes. I will defend you, and you can count on me."

Soraya, who didn't know anything about the army, was moved by their discipline and their silent

coordination. Then, to please Rabiya, she said, "When we return to the palace I will tell the old man about your courage and bravery."

The colonel smiled and said, "Lady, there is no need for that, the general knows me very well."

When Soraya heard "the general" she said, "Who is the general you are talking about?"

"General Omar, who led us to victory against the Byzantines," responded Rabiya. The widow was confused, as she didn't know who the general was. Rabiya looked at her and told her, "The one who recommended me to you."

She said with great astonishment, "What? Is there also a general involved in this undertaking?"

"No, no!" responded the colonel.

Soraya said, "Then please explain to me; I am confused. Who is the general?"

The colonel understood that she did not know that the old man was the general and said in a calm tone, "My lady, the old man who introduced you to me is General Omar."

"The old man?" the widow exclaimed.

"Yes, my lady, the old man."

Then she repeated, "He is General Omar?"

94

"Yes, my lady. You didn't know this?" Soraya was embarrassed and smiled ironically to give the impression that it was a joke on her part. The colonel smiled too and, since Soraya never made another reference to this, he never knew whether she was joking or simply tired. This new information gave her strength and courage to continue her trip under the burning sun. Although she was tired from the heat and from sitting on the horse, she didn't complain.

The colonel's family came from the northern part of Persia. His father was a rich and learned man and he gave his son Rabiya and his daughter Barka a good education. He brought a teacher from afar to teach them. It was because of his education that General Omar had chosen Rabiya as his right-hand man during the fierce battle with the Byzantines. Soraya saw that the colonel was cool-headed. Although he led the fight against the thieves with great precision and composure, Soraya was scared when all these movements were taking place. At that time she realized that she was accompanied by a man of great military skill. She was also more confident after learning that the old man was General Omar. Her doubts suddenly disappeared. She knew that Zaafer Lebranki was a politician and that the military and politicians never get along. She said to herself that her problem would be solved, *If he could beat the Byzantines, he would surely beat Zaafer Lebranki. The caliph would see clearly that Zaafer Lebranki's advice was wrong.* The

caravan moved faster now, as the colonel wanted to reach the river before sundown. The weather was clear, and a few stars could be seen in the sky. The horses too smelled the water, for they were thirsty and tired. They picked up their speed. The sun was closer to the horizon, and one could see the red sky in the west. When the colonel saw the color of the sky, he said, "My lady, do you know what the red color means at sundown?" Then he cited a proverb, "When the evening sky is red, the next day your horses could be spread."

She didn't know this and she answered, "I am not an army woman."

The colonel laughed and said, "There will never be an army woman in this area; it is against our religion."

Soraya smiled and said, "The day will come when women will learn to defend themselves."

When Rabiya heard her say this, he answered, "My lady, against whom should they defend themselves?"

She spoke spontaneously, "Against those who abuse their power."

The colonel responded in such a compassionate tone that Soraya was moved, "My lady, no one will abuse his power against a charming woman like you." He looked at her and continued, "I will defend you with my body and with my life."

Soraya realized that the colonel didn't know anything about what had happened to her son or to her. She said, "God bless men like you and like General Omar; you are our guarantors." She laughed so as not to attract any curiosity.

Rabiya laughed too and said, "Now, I have a surprise for you my lady; turn your head to the right and see for yourself."

Soraya turned her head slowly and was stunned. A beautiful landscape opened up before her eyes. The river was so wide; Soraya had never seen such a beautiful sight. She didn't realize that while she was talking with the colonel, the horses were advancing steadily. She closed her eyes as the custom was in that region, praised God, and said, "God, I pray for justice and for my son." The colonel observed her silently, touched by her faith and holiness. Although he couldn't hear what she was praying for, he could see her gesture. He had never seen a woman with such courage. In his view, she was too young to be so religious and believing. He remembered his mother when she was old; she prayed with the same gestures as Soraya. From that moment on he had great respect for Soraya. He reassured her that he would defend her by all means. General Omar had not told him who this lady was, and the colonel had not asked him. Rabiya knew only that the general selected him to

97

accompany an important lady. Soraya's conduct inspired his respect.

She was happy that, before heading west to Bousid's, she had first gone to her home and prepared all her best dresses for any occasion that might present itself. She stood still in the dark for a while, admiring the reflection of the River Euphrates. No bridge had been built to enable them to cross the river; the river was too wide for any bridge. They had to swim with their horses. Soraya had once crossed a river in the south with her father. This one looked much wider and seemed deeper. Near Baghdad there were a few barges, which transported people with their belongings. The old man had told her specifically that she had to avoid the security posts on each side of the river to avoid being seen by Zaafer Lebranki's guards. The place, which the colonel brought her to, was completely deserted.

He knew from his experience that Zaafer Lebranki's men would not likely be in such a place. Then the colonel said, "I hope, my lady that you can swim."

The lady responded, "If the horse can swim, then I can swim too."

Then the colonel graciously came up beside her and said, "My lady, whether you can swim or not, it is my duty to show you what to do. Just follow me." Then he took the bridle of his horse, lifted it to the level of his shoulder and said, "You see, my lady, do the same, and

never pull the bridle strongly. The horse has to feel that it is free; it will swim very well. But if you pull the bridle, the horse cannot breathe, and you might drown with it." The widow listened with admiration; such a lesson was needed. She was confident that she would cross the river without incident, and the fact that the colonel was crossing next to her was reassuring. After all, she was prepared to do anything to save her son.

After a short stop the colonel gave a sign to go forward. This time he deployed his men differently. Two guards had to cross first, in order to be on the other bank of the river and to make sure that no one could surprise them while they were in the water. Two advanced before the colonel and the widow, and two advanced behind the colonel. The last guards were left on the shore to protect the rear. They would cross the river only after everyone reached the other bank safely. Nothing was left to chance. The colonel had trained his guards to perfection. They obeyed him and had great respect and admiration for him since the war against the Byzantines. He was their best example, so they were prepared to do anything for him. During the war it was the colonel who penetrated the Byzantine line and freed fifty of the royal soldiers who had been captured by the Byzantines. The ten guards had been among the fifty soldiers captured by the Byzantines. They felt that they owed their life to Rabiya. They vowed to serve Colonel Rabiya as long as they lived. The widow followed the colonel, moving

slowly with her horse. She was watching him, waiting for his signal. She took off her shoes and tried to fold her long dress to her waist. When the colonel turned his head to give her the signal, he saw what she was doing and said, "My lady, there is no need for this; your dress will get wet anyway."

The widow looked at him and said, "You are right. The horse will be wet too." She gave up folding her dress. Meanwhile, the colonel caught a glimpse of her white legs. It was the first time that the colonel had seen her legs. He had never seen any woman's legs. Compared to his own skin color, Soraya's skin was very white. He was a little embarrassed for having seen her skin under her dress.

She entered the water slowly while mounted on her horse. She realized soon that her dress was already wet above her waist. She looked at the colonel, but he was advancing. She tried hard to keep her body in balance, as she couldn't hold on to the bridle. Her horse was a great swimmer; it caught up quickly with the colonel. When she saw him next to her, she said, "I am sorry, I couldn't keep up with you right away, but after a while my horse seemed to get used to me." The colonel was embarrassed; he realized that he was not in the army and that he should not have left her behind at any time, as she could have been in danger. He then slowed his horse's swimming pace, so that he could be right behind her.

That day the river was low, and once in a while the horse tripped in the river bed. Soraya almost fell into the water. Exhausted from the heat and from the long journey, she suddenly realized that the horse was already on land. Not to embarrass her, the colonel gave instructions to his guards to advance far away from the widow. As for himself, he went behind a small dune. Soraya could wring her clothes quietly, without anyone watching. After everyone had partly dried out their clothes, the colonel suggested they should eat right there and then, as they would have a long night's trip ahead. Everyone had a piece of bread and a few dates, which the chief guard had brought with him. When they had finished, the colonel gave the signal, and his small caravan continued its journey towards its destination, but, in order to avoid any encounter with the caliph's guards, the colonel chose to go a little south west, then east to rejoin the river through the desert. There he counted on the protection of the darkness of the night. When they reached the desert, Soraya had the impression that she was moving in a sea. Once in a while they encountered small caravans of camels with people that she saw for the first time. Their faces were veiled in white; they were the Bedouins from the south. The sky above them was dark; here and there she could see some stars. Only the horses' hoofbeats were heard. From time to time the colonel said something to his guards. Soraya had the feeling that she had been on the horse for a very long time. She

remembered when her father had told her one day not to sleep when she was riding on a horse. She understood now why he told her this; the rhythmical movement of the horse made her sleepy. As her back hurt, the widow stopped a few times to stretch. In order to stay awake, she also changed her position many times. Slowly, slowly, the river's noise had disappeared in the darkness. The hoofbeats of the horses was drowned by the sound of the wind, which blew from the west. After a long trip the colonel made a big detour towards the north in order to reach the river again. The desert landscape was slowly giving way to green pasture. From far away Soraya could faintly hear the bleating of sheep. She was not sure if this was really the bleating of sheep or the distant noise of the river. She knew that they were approaching an inhabited area. Then she remembered that the old man had told her to pass the first village, to continue in the same direction, and after a while she would hear the lowing of the cows. Soraya was scrutinizing the horizon, trying to discern any sign of houses in order to locate the first village. After a while she gave up and relied on the colonel's knowledge of the area. She could only see the shadow of the colonel, who once in a while told her to follow his path to avoid obstacles. She said to herself that she could never have undertaken this trip by herself; there were too many obstacles on the way; but the colonel had foreseen all of them.

Suddenly, Soraya heard the soft sound of a pipe. She tried to locate the direction from which the sound came and realized that it was Rabiya giving a signal to the guards to stop. Then each of them pulled out a white cloth from their bags. They attached them to the tails of their horses in order to be seen in the dark. Soraya had never thought about this. She was impressed to see how the colonel had a solution for every problem. Before, she had not been able to see the position of every horse in front of her. Now, it was easy to follow the path of the horses in front of her. Despite this, she did wonder how the first guard could find his way. Then she asked Rabiya, "Can you tell me how the first guard can find his way in such a dark night?" The colonel smiled, but she could not see his face. Then he said, "The guard doesn't have to see anything; the horse can see better."

The widow reacted quickly, "But how do they know the direction?"

The colonel answered, "They don't have to know the direction; I am guiding them." The widow wanted to ask how he knew the direction, but she refrained from asking Rabiya such a question, to avoid annoying him. She knew that the colonel was a smart and reliable man. She wished she could talk to him about her son, but she quickly recalled that the old man had told her not to speak about this matter with anyone except Bousid. They were moving steadily in the dark. The silence of the night

was broken by the sound of the horses' hoofbeats. Once in a while, Soraya closed her eyes. She realized that after being in the dark for a long time she had started to see. She could distinguish between the brown and the beige horses, and suddenly the beige horses became dark and the brown horses became black. She didn't know what was happening. Then she saw the horse of the colonel approaching; he seemed to be bringing her a message. His voice seemed to have changed with the quick trot of the horses. He said, "We are now just behind a small hill, and this is the best place to spend the night. We will sleep just to relax, then we will continue our journey." He deployed one of the guards on the top of the hill and the rest in the lowest part of the field around the hill. For the widow he designated the side of the hill, between himself and the guard on top of the hill. When she traveled with her father, it was always early in the morning, and never at night. But this time it was different. She was the one who had suggested riding non-stop without resting, but, after two days and two nights without rest, she realized that she was over-demanding on the men. Each hour that her son was in jail was a painful experience, but she understood that she should give them a break. She was grateful that she had the colonel as a guide and had covered a lot of ground in this short period of time. She found that the colonel was right to suggest they stop and get some rest. She finally surrendered to sleep. It was a short slumber, but it was better than nothing, and she

woke up at dawn. The colonel was awake before her. He thought to wake up the rest of the guards, but they were already waiting for him. The guards had informed him that the widow was still asleep. He approached her place slowly and said loudly to the guards, "Is everyone ready?"

Soraya got up and said, "I am not ready!"

The colonel laughed, "Take your time, my lady, we will wait for you." Soraya was relieved that they were all ready to move. She was exhausted, but she was eager to reach her destination. After she rinsed her face swiftly, she was again on her horse and quickly got used to its movement. They traveled a long distance at dawn. When the sun rose, Soraya realized that this time the sun was on her left. The colonel followed her at a small distance. Once in a while he changed his position. He moved on each side of Soraya. Around noon the colonel surprised her again.

"Look to your right." he said. The sun lit up the house of Bousid. It seemed very close, but it was still far away. The widow exclaimed, "We are there!"

The colonel reacted, "No, we are not there yet." Soraya was happy; her destination was in sight. But the guards did not slow down. They knew their way very well. The caravan was moving in a loose formation, as they were not in danger anymore. They kept the same positions. Four of the guards were still circling at a

distance around the caravan. On both sides of the path one could see the green fields. Suddenly, a small hill emerged from the sand. Soraya wondered whether it was there before, or if a sand storm had created it. The hill was like a guard protecting Bousid's village from the west. The colonel saw the hill too and said, "This is a fortress."

"I just noticed it" Soraya responded.

"This was built by the Byzantines for their defense, but we surprised them as we came from the other side," continued Rabiya.

Soraya, who seemed to be interested, asked, "And why are they keeping this fortress? Do we need it for a future war?"

The colonel answered, "No, my lady. What is good at one time is not always good." Then he picked up a handful of dirt and said, "You see, this dirt is not from this region; it was transported from another part of the country." In fact, the soil of this region was darker and the one the Byzantines brought is sandy. When they reached the giant hill, the fortress looked different. The artificial structure looked much bigger in size; it was impressive and imposing. It was built to contain three thousand Byzantine fighters; close up, it was overwhelming.

"The general used to spend a lot of time on top of the hill. He liked to survey all the fields belonging to his son. This fortress was the main source of his son's fortune; he inherited the entire land that is today in his possession. When General Omar won the final battle against the Byzantines, the caliph was so pleased with the general's performance, that he donated an entire lot of land to him and his family. This is how the caliph had read the donation at that time, 'I, the Caliph of Baghdad and King of the Persian Empire, herewith declare that, in recognition of General Omar's excellent leadership, which has led to victory against the Byzantine army, I herewith donate the fortress built by the enemy's army, and all the surrounding land within one day's horse ride from each side of the fortress, to General Omar and all his heirs for all time.' The declaration was signed and sealed by the caliph of Baghdad and king of the Persian Empire." The widow enjoyed listening to the account of Bousid's fortune. This news had reassured her that Bousid was rich and that he could afford to give her the thousand and one camels. The colonel had again proved a good source of information.

The widow, for her own reasons, wanted to spend some time familiarizing herself with the fortress. She said to herself, *I will have more to say if I know the history and have seen the fortress.*

107

As she was busy with herself, a guard runner came towards her and said, "We have found two men on horses moving in our territory. Should we kill them?"

The widow, all confused, thinking that the guard was talking to her, said, "No, don't kill them! Ask them what they want!"

The colonel who was caught in-between, answered, "My lady, I am sorry for the confusion." Then he addressed the guards as follows, "Attach them on their horses and bring them with us to Bousid's village."

The widow was happy that he was not going to kill them and said, "What will you do with them?"

The colonel responded, "We will keep them in the village until you meet Bousid and get back to the palace. I don't want any surprise; they could well be the agents of Zaafer Lebranki."

When she heard the name of Zaafer Lebranki, the widow was more responsive to the argument of the colonel than of the two men. She smiled and said, "Colonel, I am sorry; I hope I didn't undermine your plan or your authority."

Rabiya was calm and answered with a faint smile, "No, no! Would you still like to see the fortress?"

"Oh yes, of course!" responded Soraya in a firm tone. The colonel made a sign to his guard to change the plan.

The guard reacted immediately. They deployed themselves towards the fortress and checked every corner and every hiding place; then they made a sign to Rabiya that the fortress was safe. All these movements gave Soraya a valuable experience; she had no knowledge of military matters. But now she felt that, between the general, the colonel and the caliph, she had to show interest in these subjects. Her father had never taught her anything about war or the army. He wanted to spare her such knowledge. He used to say, "The army is a matter for men and not for women." Soraya remembered her father's words very well. She wished she knew more, but she was thankful to have men like the general and the colonel on her side.

When Soraya was young, she saw how her father gave away her sister to a rich old man with a handshake. This way her sister Leila had to marry an old man. She never forgave him for that. But, as revenge, Leila educated her sister Soraya not to follow her path and to find a husband herself. Soraya loved her cousin, who later became her husband. She had the courage to marry him without the consent of her father. This was due to her sister Leila. She was also the one who financed Soraya when her husband died. In fact, Leila was enjoying helping Soraya as she shared her story with her. Now that both men had died, the two sisters shared a new house in the newly built Baghdad. They had a comfortable life; they had all the money they needed. But all the money in the world

could not buy them all the camels the caliph had ordered her to bring as a ransom for her son. Soraya did not tell her sister about this entire episode. She thought that she could solve the problem by herself. When the caravan reached the fortress, the widow exclaimed, "How huge this construction is! It is incredible how much dirt and sand the Byzantines brought here." The fortress had the shape of a horseshoe with forty steps leading to the top. After the last step of the stairs there was a gangway protected by a wall of stone, which ran to all the battle stations. The height was equal to a three-story building and the width was approximately five hundred and fifty feet. The colonel was happy to see the widow showing interest in the fortress. He was next to her at all times to answer any questions she might have. When they were on the top of the fortress, Soraya asked, "Why did the Byzantines need this height?"

The colonel was ready for her, "My lady, how far can you see from here?"

Soraya answered, "Very far, to the next village."

"You see, you answered your own question. The Byzantines wanted to control the entire region, so if an army was moving, they could spot it beforehand. This way they would avoid any surprise attack."

Soraya smiled with a faint charm and said, "But you told me that we had surprised them. How?"

The colonel reacted quickly, "Yes, we surprised them at night."

Soraya laughed aloud, saying, "That is smart! And they didn't think about the night?"

"No!" answered Rabiya without any further comment. After a while the colonel and the widow left the fortress and went directly towards Bousid's village, as the sun was almost setting.

"It would be dangerous to walk or to ride at night in the village. All the villagers' dogs will be free until the morning," said the colonel. Knowing the rules of the village, Rabiya sent one of the guards to inform Bousid about their arrival and to hand him a letter from his father, General Omar. The colonel's guard also handed over the two prisoners to Bousid's guards. He wanted to enter the village at night so that the darkness would protect them from the curiosity of the inhabitants.

When they entered the village, there were no dogs to be seen, but their barking resounded loudly. From time to time a cat jumped and passed between the horses and created a little disturbance. Once in a while they passed a house with a dim light. The villagers didn't seem to sleep. The lowing of the cows created a kind of rhythm.

"This village seems to be a rich one," said the widow.

The colonel heard what she was saying, and continued, "It is the richest village in the entire empire."

The widow nodded as a sign of satisfaction. She was happy that this village was prosperous. Then she murmured, *To get one thousand and one camels, it has to be a wealthy village.* This thought eased her concern. *After such a long trip, I have to be successful,* she said to herself. *If not, how could I ever forgive myself for wasting such precious time while my son is suffering in jail?* All these thoughts went through her mind while she was riding.

From a distance, a large house emerged amongst all the village houses. It looked like a palace. It had two entrances in the front, one door, and one gate for the carriages. When she saw the size of the house, she was comforted, as she knew she was dealing with a rich and respectable man. Now it was just a question of a few days and all the trouble would disappear. But no one could hear her thoughts. The colonel changed his position in his caravan. All the guards surrounded the colonel and the widow in a much tighter circle, so as to give them more protection when they entered Bousid's territory. Now the responsibility for their security was on Bousid's guards. When they reached the big white house, the position changed again: the colonel was now in the front, the widow behind him, and all the guards formed a half circle behind them. Bousid was already outside, in front of the gate, ready to greet them, as was the custom when a dignitary arrived in his village. After he greeted them all, the neighbors came out and applauded them. The

women of the village had come forward and performed a dance of the region. The widow was pleased and felt for the first time that someone cared about her. She addressed Bousid and the villagers with these words, "Sir Bousid, noble people, you are the guarantee of our nation! Thank God for giving us a generous and noble family like the El Hallalis, which gave us General Omar El Hallali and his son Bousid El Hallali." Everyone applauded her, she waved with her scarf, then Bousid opened the gate for her to enter with her horse, and the colonel with his guards followed her. The gate was closed behind them by Bousid's guards. The colonel went directly to his usual guest quarters, the guards went with Bousid's guards, and the widow followed Bousid El Hallali who was joined by his wife Farida. Together they went to Bousid's private quarters. He had received many dignitaries in his marvelous residence. Once they entered Bousid's private room, he excused himself and let his wife show Soraya her suite. Farida had always taken care of the lady guests. On the outside she appeared to be a gracious host, but she had always feared the presence of any woman. Her husband was an honest and generous man and he never gave her any excuse to be jealous. But in that part of the world, where a simple pretext means an automatic divorce, Farida wanted to protect her interests. First she sat with Soraya in the suite, so as to get the maximum of information about her.

Soraya didn't divulge anything to Farida, neither the reason for her coming there, nor who she was.

Soraya remembered the words of the old man who told her, "Do not tell anyone your story, only to Bousid."

If the old man had not meant "only to Bousid", he could have mentioned his wife Farida, had he chosen, she murmured to herself. After a first chat, Farida had a good impression of Soraya, but as usual she never trusted anyone and especially someone who looked as nice and educated as Soraya. The truth is that Soraya's charm and beauty were unique and that she spoke with a sweet feminine voice, which added brilliance to her eloquent language. She had inherited this talent from her father, who was a great speaker. Bousid was taken by her beauty and by her black eyes, which looked like a deep well. When he read his father's secret letter that the colonel had forwarded to him through one of his guards prior to his arrival, and before he had a chance to see Soraya, Bousid was shocked and astonished by the caliph's behavior, but when he saw her, he said to himself, *If my father gave this lady his horse and delegated his best men to accompany her, it is no wonder. She really deserves to live in a palace and to have a king for a husband.* But he wanted to appear like a real El Hallali. General Omar knew what he was doing by choosing Bousid and not his brothers. He knew that Bousid was an honorable man and that he had more qualities than his

114

brothers. He was wise, calm, and showed great patience and compassion for others. He could listen for hours to anyone his father would send to him. He realized that in order to be just, he first had to understand the problem. He was a charming and elegant host. Bousid never disappointed his father; he had always shown respect for him and for the caliph. The colonel had been his guest many times over the years, and they got along well. The colonel was like a brother to Bousid, and he knew that he could count on Bousid when it was needed.

Bousid went with the colonel and sat down with him for tea, as he wanted to have the colonel's first-hand report of his father's health and well-being, and to have the first impression and evaluation from the colonel, who had traveled with the lady and had seen her in many different situations. Bousid was wondering whether the widow had any less than perfect side. Everything he heard from the colonel was excellent; he himself had a good first impression, too. Neither the colonel nor Bousid knew the real reason behind her coming, nor anything about her request. But General Omar, whose father was from a noble Arabian family, had sympathy for Soraya's plight. He knew that her husband and her father were also from a noble Arabian family. He was pleased that she was not prepared to break the vow that she had given to her late husband. When the general learned the whole story, he said to himself, *This is pure Arabian blood!*

115

Soraya's husband had told her when he was alive, "Do not dishonor my son and our family with other than pure Arabian origin." But she couldn't give this excuse to Harun Al-Rashid. She knew very well that he came from the Al Abbasid dynasty, which was a Persian dynasty. Harun Al-Rashid himself didn't care. His first wife was from an Arabian family. His second wife was a Persian woman. Harun Al-Rashid had met her while he was traveling. All this information was unknown to Bousid. The colonel too didn't know about Harun Al-Rashid's and Farha's backgrounds. Rabiya himself was from a noble Persian family. After all, it was a delicate matter, but the old man well knew how to balance everything. Despite his Arabian background, he was very loyal to the king. After dinner, Bousid asked his wife and the servant to leave him alone with Soraya. In the secret letter, his father asked Bousid to explain to her all the ramifications and the background of everyone, so that she might understand the Arabian implications. As soon as he was alone with Soraya, Bousid began, "My father asked me in his note to tell you all the truth. You are, as my father let me know, of Arabian Muslim origin like us."

Soraya was speechless, but relieved that she was in good Arabian hands. Now she understood why the old man was so eager to help her.

Then Bousid continued, "The general wants you to know all about the caliph and Zaafer Lebranki. The caliph mistrusts his closest adviser, Zaafer Lebranki, despite the fact that he is Persian like him. He grew up in the palace when the caliph was young. He was there because of his father Yahya, who had been the caliph's father's adviser. In fact, Harun Al-Rashid didn't choose Zaafer Lebranki; he inherited him with the court."

General Omar knew all this. That was the reason why he was always close to the caliph and had free access to the palace. The Persian dynasties had created this mixture of Persian and Arabian subjects; it was the best way to secure their reign; and, to make things more complicated, they had created the town of Baghdad. This was a way to acquire the loyalty of the Arabs. But Harun Al-Rashid's father was smart not to build his palace in the new town of Baghdad; instead, he built it in the eastern outskirts and facing the Persian mountains. In the event of an Arab revolt, it would be easy for the king to cross over to the other side of the mountains. But this was Harun Al-Rashid's father's point of view. Harun Al-Rashid was well beloved by the Arab inhabitants for his courageous fight against the Byzantines. In the event of any trouble, the dynasty had always one party on its side, either the Persians, or the Arabs. His empire extended from the Mediterranean Sea to India. The Muslims were grateful to him for spreading Islam throughout his entire empire. Although he was the leader of the faithful, he

himself was not religious, but no one knew how deep his belief was. The caliph didn't know from where the widow came. He didn't have the time or the patience to ask or to inquire about her. His love was a spontaneous one.

Bousid spoke openly with Soraya and told her, "I know exactly why my father sent you here. I have already given instructions to assemble one thousand and one female camels all one year old and in all the existing colors." He looked at her with kindness and continued, "But you have to be patient and you have to stay with us for a couple of weeks, as most of the camels are coming from the south and the larger part are coming from Arabia."

The widow, who had not even had the time to tell her story, was happily surprised to learn in a wonderful way that her wish was granted. Bousid was about to continue talking when Soraya interjected, "May I say thank you for your kindness and for your understanding of my plight." Bousid lightly waved his hand, as if ignoring the words of thanks, and said, "Koolu min Allah," as the Arab custom prescribed, which means "Everything is from God." In the Arab tradition, all praise and thanks should be directed toward God. Bousid was very humble, but she knew from her father that if someone comes to your house, he is considered to be the guest of the Prophet, and whatever he asks for, he should get.

Now Soraya would have an answer for the caliph and particularly for his adviser, Zaafer Lebranki. She was so happy, that she could not contain herself, and said, "Allah karim ma'a el Arab." (God is generous with the Arabs.)

Bousid was taken by her joy too, and felt that she filled the room with happiness. He smiled and let her enjoy herself. He handed her a cup of tea and waited for a while, then he continued, "We are the guardians of our religion. My father had convinced the caliph not only to unify all the Muslims, but to promote Islam everywhere in the empire. He was also the architect behind the expression that said, 'Those who die in combat go straight to heaven', and he made clear that combat was not physical combat or war, but the struggle within ourselves, of which most Muslims do not understand the meaning. If you are consistent in your struggle, you will be victorious in every way. The caliph understood the value of this union, and he also understood that it was in his interest to do so."

While he was talking, the widow was very impressed. She was mostly astonished by the old man and the way he was communicating with his son from a distance. She found the father and the son both intelligent and pleasant company. At this point, Soraya could see a change in her destiny, and she thanked her husband in her heart for sending her such a noble helper. Now she felt that she

could sleep quietly for the first time since her encounter with the king. She also knew that the old man had stayed close to the palace and that he would probably relieve her son from the hardship he was subjected to. He had enormous influence in the palace. If Zaafer Lebranki had known with whom he was dealing, he would not have started at all. In the past he had learned a lesson when he embarrassed a nobleman without knowing that he was the closest friend of the general. Zaafer Lebranki had risked his entire career, but at that time he apologized to General Omar. He had to promise not to do anything in the future without first checking with him. Since then, he had lost a lot of his authority to the general. Soraya was pleased to hear this last sentence from Bousid. This evening had brought her a feeling of great salvation. She would have the camels, and she had acquired a great deal of knowledge. Bousid and his father were a blessing to her. Soraya could not have dreamed of returning to the palace with such a history lesson. She praised God in her heart for this entire episode. She and her son would come out of it with a lot of strength and with wisdom. When Bousid finished speaking, he said to her, "My lady, I hope this has not been boring for you; you must be very tired from the long journey."

"Yes," responded Soraya, I'd better go to sleep."

"You are right," replied Bousid, for we do not have a lot of time before us." Then, with a firm gesture, he

clapped his hands, as was the practice in that region, for the servant to come and accompany Soraya to her room. When Soraya was finally in her room, after a long and moving day, she was exhausted but happy. That night she slept like a child. She woke up with the rooster's crow. But, as no one came to wake her up, she stayed in her bed until late in the morning.

The noises of the village were different from the noises of the city. She could hear the first arrival of camels from the neighboring village. Her problem had created enormous activity in Bousid's village and in the surrounding area. Mokhtar, Bousid's son, was among the first to be sent to the south and to Arabia to procure camels. Soraya did not have a chance to make his acquaintance. Before noon, Bousid's wife arrived, accompanied by a servant with a platter full of cheese, butter, milk and home-made flat bread. The smell of the bread whetted Soraya's appetite. She was happy to be treated like a dignitary, although she hadn't known anyone just a few days earlier. The first day, she didn't see Bousid at all. He was probably busy assembling camel herds. Through the shutters of her window she could see the men working hard. There were men on horses everywhere, moving from one place to another. Soraya decided to mark every passing day on a branch of a tree in the middle of the courtyard of Bousid's house. When the marks reached the end of the wood, it was twenty one days since she had arrived in Bousid's

village. Bousid's wife Farida took Soraya out a few times on horseback, showing her their great village and their fields. Farida never asked Soraya about her presence in her house or about her mission. She knew that, when the general sent someone to Bousid's house, it was always for a special reason. She kept her feelings to herself, but the presence of such a beautiful lady had intrigued her.

When she heard from the village that her husband was to assemble such a great number of camels, she was not happy, as she thought about the immense fortune that her husband was about to give to Soraya, but as a woman she could not know the purpose of these camels. After all, Bousid had not known this lady before. Farida could not understand the reason for Soraya's coming to their village. Bousid gave her hospitality; he fed her and fed her guards with her; he also fed all the camel drivers, whom he had assembled from everywhere, until the day of departure. In the end, Farida was furious and upset with her husband, but she never told him anything. She preferred to wait until her son's return from the south. It was not the first time that Bousid had given a large donation to a stranger, but this time she thought that her husband was about to make an enormous mistake, and that he might lose all the fortune he had worked for. Every day hundreds of carts loaded with straw and food for the camels rolled to a field. On the last day, early in the morning, the herd stood assembled outside the village in a huge field next to a small creek. This

adventure must have cost Bousid a fortune, but he did it with his noble heart. He kept saying, "We have to straighten out this injustice with fairness and charity."

The general had explained everything to Bousid in his long letter written in Arabic. In one sentence he had said, "We have to protect our caliph from Zaafer Lebranki's bad advice. Even if it costs us a fortune, it will be worth it. Do not forget where our wealth came from." These words said everything to Bousid. His wife could not understand all the ramifications. She never knew where Bousid's fortune came from. She would never know the real reason for this great undertaking. Even if Bousid were to explain it to her, she would never understand, as she came from a poor village and had never been to any school.

*

A few days after Soraya had left Al-Rashid's palace to go to see Bousid, General Omar had visited the caliph to see how he was doing. As the caliph was in a good mood, the old man didn't miss the opportunity to talk with him about the widow's son, knowing that Zaafer Lebranki was fully occupied with his security, trying to find out where the widow had gone and where she could possibly find such a huge number of camels. He was curious to know, who was the rich man who could finance such an undertaking? His security guards lost the trace of the widow, and two of their best security men

were reported missing. The general suggested the following to the caliph, "Let the youth out of the jail. For security, you can hold him in the palace, and he can meanwhile keep your daughter company. After all, he is a very well educated young man. If the widow returns empty-handed, she will be happy to see how generous you are, and how you took care of her dear son. Just this fact will make her love you. That of course is if she cannot find the thousand and one camels you have imposed on her."

The caliph was happy to hear the general's advice and responded, "That is the best advice I have heard this week. The widow will know that I am a compassionate man, and as I am sure she will never find the number of camels I have fined her - at least not in our region - she will be more compliant than she was before."

The general smiled and said, "Your Majesty, you know me, but please let me tell you that no matter who gave you the advice of the fine, it was the worst advice I have ever heard. Not only will it give you a bad reputation among kings of other nations, but first and foremost it will certainly not gain you the widow's appreciation."

"Indeed, indeed! Let's hope that this time everything will end well," the king responded.

"Let's hope, my dear caliph, that this incident will not tarnish your good reputation as the victorious king," added the general.

When the caliph heard the words "as the victorious king," he was moved and answered as follows, "I should have asked you for advice; you have never disappointed me; the opposite, you brought victory to your country, to your people, and above all to the entire empire." The next day, Rahman, the widow's son, was released with an apology from the caliph, and he was told that he had to stay in the palace until his mother would return from her voyage. Rahman didn't trust anyone. When he was introduced to Princess Khayet, he set a secret agenda for himself. He said to himself, *Let her suffer like my mother!* This thought directed his actions until the general had the chance to speak with him alone. He told him the entire story. Rahman was wise and somehow trusted the general. He stayed in the palace not far away from Khayet's quarters and, as the days passed, she developed a fine feeling for Rahman, which caused her to dream every night about him. He liked her too, but he didn't want his feelings to betray his love for his mother. His attitude made Khayet more eager to be with him.

Rahman was indeed a well-educated young man. He never showed any warm feelings or any antipathy towards Khayet. When his grandfather was alive, he had seen to it that Rahman would be well educated and had

125

paid for good teachers to come every week to teach him manners, behavior and diplomacy. His wish was that Rahman would become an ambassador. Rahman had the chance to study, besides Arabic, which was his mother tongue, the Persian language and the most known Indian dialects spoken among the diplomatic community. Rahman did not hide his sadness from Khayet, but she ascribed his behavior to her father's action, having put him in jail without any reason. She decided to be patient with him until his mother's return. She too was worried about Rahman's mother and was scared that something could happen to her. She saw her love and her dream disappear and feared that her destiny would be changed with such guilt.

The caliph, Khayet and Zaafer Lebranki were the only ones who did not know the whereabouts of the widow. Rahman knew the entire story from the general. He too had to wait patiently for his mother's arrival, but he never showed any sign of worry. The caliph admired Rahman's attitude and education and had included him among his short list of potential husbands for his daughter. All these thoughts assumed that Soraya would return safe and without the camels.

Zaafer Lebranki was nervous and very concerned about the fate of the widow and particularly for her safety. He didn't forget that he had been the one who had advised the king. He realized that his advice was not as

good as he had thought. He became more worried about the fact that the general had freed Rahman, in his absence, without waiting for his return. He remembered well that in the past the general had warned him not to challenge him. Seeing that both Khayet and Rahman got along well, Zaafer Lebranki realized the failure of his entire plan. The only chance he now had was to try minimizing the damage, and to hope that the widow would return safely, so her son could see her again. Contrary to his original plan, which he had proposed to the king, he now hoped, for his own sake, that the widow would find the camels and that she would be able to honor the king's demand. If the widow did not find the camels, as he believed, she would then be the queen. Zaafer Lebranki had not thought thoroughly about that when he gave his advice to the king. Foremost he wanted to calm the king's pain at that moment. The only way not to be punished for his advice would be if the widow had a safe and successful return.

*

Let us now return to Soraya and to Bousid's village. Never before had Bousid's village or the surrounding villages seen such a large herd. Bousid had undertaken the biggest enterprise in his life. When the camels passed next to Bousid's house, the ground shook as though there were an earthquake. Soraya was trying to visualize how this huge herd would shake Baghdad and the palace. The

caliph would be amazed! He would learn the meaning and the power of a loyal woman. Zaafer Lebranki would never forget the lesson he would receive from an honest woman. In fact, she was right in her thinking; they would learn the value of a good woman, and they would never challenge a resolute lady like Soraya ever again. That was what Soraya was thinking.

The village had been transformed into a huge animal marketplace. The entire region was aware of Bousid's strength and now, through the very scene of these camels, the esteem and respect for Bousid and his father, General Omar, would increase considerably. Finally, the day arrived for the colonel to start the return journey.

After helping the widow pack her belongings, Farida was more jealous than ever, since she had seen the kind of clothes and other belongings that Soraya had in her possession. Only a princess could wear such clothes. Farida said to herself, *I hope that my son will soon return home from his long trip.* As she was looking at the widow's luggage, she hoped to be able to convince her son to return all the wealth his father was giving to the widow.

Meanwhile, Soraya was ready to depart. She asked Farida to assemble all the servants and before leaving she looked everyone in the eye and said, "Good-bye, you Arab people of Bousid's village. What you are seeing today is nothing compared to what the Almighty is

preparing for you." Then she looked Farida in the eye and said, "I thank you and especially your generous husband. I pray to Allah for your safety and your health." Bousid had provided her with one of his horses. She mounted it, and was on her way, with all the camels the king had asked for. She could not have dreamed to be in possession of such a herd. As before, the colonel was in charge of the widow's security. Bousid advised him to disguise himself, so as not to be recognized by Zaafer Lebranki's guards. Colonel Rabiya instructed his guards, who were in charge of the security of the herd and of the camel drivers, neither to divulge the source of the herd, nor to talk about Bousid's village, in order not to compromise his father. This was the reason why Bousid had given her a different horse. Her entrance into Baghdad on General Omar's horse would compromise the entire scheme.

The widow was moving at a steady pace, but was still not far from the village. She was wondering about this entire venture and couldn't comprehend how her destiny had brought her to the general and to his son. Everything seemed like a dream to her.

Now while the herd was slowly moving away from the village, Bousid's son Mokhtar had finally returned from the south. He was tired and dirty from the long journey. He was the one who had brought most of the camels. His uncle from Arabia was the one who helped

him assemble the herd and the camel drivers. As soon as Mokhtar entered the house, his mother received him with a cry and complained as follows, "My dear son, you don't know the story. Your father has given our fortune to the lady who came charming him; he fell into her trap like a cow in front of a butcher. We will soon be poor, and you will be begging the neighbors for money. That's what your father wants for you!"

Mokhtar saw his mother crying as on the day she lost her father, and told her, "My dear mother, I came burning and sweating from the desert and your words are strong; they stung me like a whip; they added fire to my burning heart! I will soon ride on my horse and bring back all that my father has given away. Please, mother, do not cry!" Then he quickly washed himself, jumped on his horse and rode off at lightning speed. He had the best horse in the village. The horse's galloping steps attracted Bousid' attention. He asked one of the servants where his son was heading.

From afar the widow saw a horse coming towards her and said to herself, *Only leaders and men of determination can ride that fast!* She could not recognize the man from that distance, but her instinct and intelligence let her deduce that he could only be Bousid himself or one of his sons, who probably wanted to see her before her departure. She stopped and made a sign to the colonel to stop too. She had prepared herself to give

him a cordial greeting. When Mokhtar was but a short distance from her, she gave cheers. When she could see his face, she smiled and said, "God give you more riches, you noble and generous man!"

When Mokhtar heard these words and saw her beauty, he said loudly, "The generous give away precious stones at their highest value, and the stingy do not even give a drop of water from their goatskin. My father gave one thousand and one camels from our estate and I am adding my best horse to it. Please add my horse to your caravan, my lady. Continue your trip and God be with you!"

"Life belongs to you, son of purity," responded Soraya. Mokhtar was applauded by all the camel drivers and the security people. In that region generosity is one of the greatest virtues. After handing his horse to the lady, he returned on foot.

Bousid, who was alarmed by the noise of the horse, questioned one of his loyal servants, and she told him the entire story about his wife setting up his son against him. He took his sword and went to the top of a hill overlooking the entire valley with the intention of killing his son if he returned with the herd. He said to himself, *If my son brings back the herd, this would mean that he is not my legitimate son, and that his mother has not been faithful to me.* These were his thoughts. Then he waited patiently on the hill. Bousid had to wait much longer than he had expected. Mokhtar was already tired from his trip,

and now, as he had to walk, he was dragging his feet and moving slowly, slowly. As Bousid thought that something had happened to his son, he took his horse and a second horse and went toward him. When he was just a few feet away from him, he saw the exhaustion in his son's eyes. Sweat covered his face. Bousid was amazed to see his son in such a state and said, "What happened, my son?"

Mokhtar responded, "Father, I am sorry, I could not help it. When I saw the wondrous lady, I gave her my horse too, I hope you will not be angry."

The father was so happy that his face lit up with joy, and he said, "You are my real son; you are a giver and not a receiver."

That day, Bousid declared a village feast in honor of his son. Then he brought two witnesses home with him, as it was customary in that part of the world, and swore, as the Muslim law prescribes, "Bel haram," which means "defiled". His wife was officially declared a divorced woman. He gave all his remaining fortune to his son and said, "My son, I don't need anything else. I will live with you in my quarters." Mokhtar was touched by his father's generosity and his immense love. He did not offer any resistance to his father for having divorced his mother; he understood that his mother's complaints were unjustified. Bousid did not deprive his wife of anything; he gave her a house, ten cows, three horses and a hundred

132

sheep. He also delegated to her ten of his men and two of his security guards. He gave instructions to his son to pay her every year, by way of a pension, ten percent of his harvest.

For the son this was an important lesson. Although he loved his mother, he found her behavior unacceptable when she wanted to reverse her husband's generous action. Not only did he not blame his father for having divorced her, but he was prepared to do the same if something like this ever happened to him. He could not understand why his mother had become so upset about the poor widow. But he knew that his mother had come from different traditions and customs than his father.

After two days of sleeping and relaxing, he sat with his father and gave him a final report about all the people he met in the south and in Arabia. He recounted how everyone received him and the kind of reception they had prepared for him. Mokhtar was very meticulous; he had a good character. He also prepared a financial report to show to whom he had given more money and to whom he had given less. When his father asked him why he gave less to one than to another, he responded, "Those who gave their camels with generosity received more money, and those who were hesitant, he felt that they didn't deserve it." Bousid enjoyed listening to his son; he was very pleased to see that his son knew how to judge and how he elaborated the entire episode without

leaving anything out. After all, it was a large enterprise that he had undertaken. Then he thought about how his grandfather would be proud of him.

Chapter 8

Back To Baghdad

Soraya could not forget the young Mokhtar, who was so generous and gave her his horse on top of all the fortune his father had already given. She felt sorry that he had to return on foot. He looked nice and his eyes were black like the sky on a winter night. She promised herself to do everything that lay in her power to find him a nice and decent woman. She wished she had a daughter. When she reached the Byzantine fort, she climbed her way up to the top and once again admired the view. It was so splendid; no one had ever seen such a panorama with so many camels moving. It looked like waves of water advancing slowly. She had the impression she was watching a sea with many brown waves. One could see the shape changing with every movement of the herd, and the color of the camels looked like a marker on the ground, which was changing minute by minute. While she was observing her huge herd, she was at the same time thinking of the face of Harun Al-Rashid. She smiled discreetly about her thoughts. The colonel enjoyed seeing her in a good mood. From his position he was

deliberating with himself on the purpose of this entire enterprise. For it to be a private project was out of question. The general would not have put his mind to it if this were not a state affair. He couldn't figure out what the general had in mind when he asked him to undertake such a trip. *This is certainly a strategy of the general to use camels instead of horses; it must be a new diversionary tactic.* Such a large number of camels would certainly be needed for a huge military campaign, but he could not figure out against whom this huge power could be directed. However, he was certain that the general would tell him, as usual, in due time. It was a habit of the general never to tell his strategy to anyone, even to his best officer. He always made sure that every single detail was meticulously taken care of when he prepared a campaign. But before any attack, he would assemble all the high-ranking officers and explain what he had in mind, and he would always ask if they understood. He had learned from the various campaigns with the general that he had to be patient and ask any questions only at the end. Then the general has never hidden anything from him.

Rabiya admired Soraya's courage and her perseverance. He was finally happy for being associated with such a huge and secret undertaking. Ever since he was put in charge of Soraya's security, he had been unable to find out who she was, and he did not dare ask any questions, lest he appear overly curious. From her

136

behavior, he assumed that she was very important and maybe an ally from a neighboring country. He abandoned this thought, as he believed that soon he would know the entire story. Nor did the widow ever tell him about the purpose of her undertaking. He respected her for this. Just when he was prepared to call her, she was on her way down from the fortress. He ran up the stairs to be at her service.

When she saw him coming at such a speed, she told him, "Colonel, do you believe that such a number of camels could be found in this area?"

The colonel was surprised by her question, and did not know what to answer. He thought that the time had arrived, and that she was now prepared to tell him the entire purpose of her mission. Then in a serious tone he said, "My lady, honestly, no." He added, "It is frightening to see such an ocean of camels. The sheer numbers can change the balance of power in any given battle."

These words pleased Soraya; she realized that, coming from a professional military man like the colonel, they had to be true. She responded calmly, "Yes, you are right. With this herd I will have the power to change many things."

Such a statement, coming from her, is worth a lot, murmured Rabiya. Then he said to himself, *I was right, it is a question of power.* He only hoped now, that she

would choose him for the big task. He avoided asking any questions, as he did not want to appear foolish. He was grateful to the general, who had called him for this mission.

Now it was a question of time, but he was puzzled about the reason behind the decision to move the herd into the city. He tried to figure out the caliph's scheme. Then he murmured to himself, *The caliph certainly wanted to let the enemy know about the power he had. It could also be a scare tactic or a diversion maneuver. In any case, the number of camels is so big, that no matter what the caliph's purpose is, it will certainly fulfill the task.* These were Colonel Rabiya's thoughts. He wanted to avoid reaching the river at the same time as the herd. He conferred with Soraya, and suddenly their horses made a very large detour at a speed known only in a battle. He wanted to cross the river before anyone else. When they reached the river, it was almost dark. Then he asked the widow if she did not mind crossing the river right then, or if she preferred waiting until the morning.

The widow answered with a firm voice, "Who cares about the night? We should move as quickly as possible." She seemed to act like a general or a queen. Before even waiting for the colonel to answer, she ran with her horse and was soon in the middle of the river.

The colonel was surprised by her reaction and her resolve. He followed her at a distance. When she reached

the other bank of the river, the colonel was almost in the middle. This time she had an edge, and the colonel was embarrassed for being caught by surprise. When he too reached the other bank of the river, he smiled and said, "Congratulations, you did it alone!"

The widow understood that she had infringed on his authority. After all, he was in charge of her security. With a charming smile, she said to him, "I almost lost control of my horse, I was happy that you were behind me." This sounded almost apologetic from a lady whom the colonel respected very much.

He had preferred to be embarrassed rather than notice any weakening in her attitude and her behavior. But he was also very well educated and understood that Soraya had respect for him. He appreciated her sharpness and replied, "No, my lady! You control your horse very well. I like your determination."

Soraya, realizing that she had started a duet of pleasant words, said, "You are the leader of this trip; you are in charge!" The colonel was happy. Deep in his heart, these words sounded like an order and an answer to his wish. It sounded to him like a hint of some sort. She may have chosen him for the future task. He looked more composed and gave his horse a signal that he used in the army. Soraya noticed that she was dealing with a strong and capable man. She wanted to strengthen his position,

and in a firm tone she told him, "Colonel, if it is alright with you, I will call you 'my colonel'."

The colonel was thrilled to hear this from Soraya. He was sure now that she was preparing him to be her colonel. Or, what she may have meant by calling him "my colonel" was that she intended to be closer to him. Either interpretation pleased Colonel Rabiya.

Meanwhile, all the guards had joined Soraya and Rabiya. This time he used a different path from the one he took on his way to the village. Rabiya was the one who chose quarters suitable for a lady. This time Soraya did not wish to be separated from the security guards. She called the colonel and told him that she did not mind being with everyone, as she now considered the colonel and the guards as part of her camp.

The colonel could not expect better from such a lady, and he answered, "As you wish, my lady, I am your humble servant." These words let her know that he accepted her authority. Now he tried to figure out from which neighboring country the danger could be expected. He upgraded his prior evaluation and was confident now, that he was dealing with a queen. He tried to remember every gesture and every word that she had spoken. He regretted that the general had not told him anything about her, but he trusted him with his life.

Chapter 9

Zaafer Lebranki and His Security

None of Zaafer Lebranki's security forces managed to locate the widow, or even to get a hint as to where she could be. His secret service lost her trail, and as the caliph was impatient to know where the widow was, Zaafer Lebranki assured him of the soundness of his strategy and that his forces had surrounded the widow and were on the verge of knowing every move she would make. This was the version of the story that Zaafer Lebranki told the caliph. In fact, he lied. He was swimming in a dark sea and didn't know the widow's plan or her whereabouts. All that Zaafer Lebranki remembered was her firm tone when she spoke to the caliph. He knew he would have a problem with her. He preferred not to take any risks anymore and gave instructions to his security people to close the four city gates. General Omar was fully aware of Zaafer Lebranki's plan and had secretly sent a runner with a good horse to alert the colonel, and to give him some instructions as to how to proceed further. It was a quiet night, and the herd was to cross the river early in the

morning. That day the colonel was awakened by the noise of the horse's footbeat. His guards had intercepted the rider before reaching the colonel or Soraya's camp. The guards brought the intruder to the colonel, and they soon realized that the man's face had been wounded and that he had blood all over his clothes. The wounded rider was the general's messenger. He brought with him a scroll hidden in his undershirt. The colonel knew who this man was and asked him, "What happened to you?"

The messenger almost fainted. The guard gave him water, and only after that did he start to talk, "The gates of the city are heavily guarded, but the western gate has only a token guard. The general wanted me to pass through the eastern gate, which had a very heavy guard. I jumped over the head of the guards with my horse, and I fell on my head, but I managed to catch my horse and escape. I didn't stop, since the general wanted me to attract the guards' attention. He had something in mind."

The colonel was standing next to the widow, and both were listening to the brave young messenger. The colonel ordered his guards to give him the daily ration of food and water. The messenger refreshed himself, and was ready to return if necessary. Rabiya carefully read the general's message, which said, "Soraya should enter the city with my messenger. She should be disguised as a peasant. The disguise is in the bundle carried by the messenger. Take a few extra camel riders, after

thoroughly checking them yourself. These riders will enter through the northern gate, you and your guards will enter through the southern gate, and a few hundred camels should enter from the northern and the eastern gates. One hundred camels should be ready to move at approximately one hour intervals from the western gate. Prepare the rest of the camels to be ready to move at approximately two hour intervals from the southern gate, which is now heavily guarded. As soon as the first camel enters the northern gate, you will give the go-ahead to the rest of the herd to move forward." Meanwhile the widow had disguised herself in the peasant clothes, as the general had instructed, and she rode with two horse riders. They were also disguised as peasants, but in fact they were the best guards the colonel had. The messenger could not go with Soraya, as his wound might have attracted the curiosity of Zaafer Lebranki's security guards.

When Soraya reached the gate, the security guards were still drinking their tea and were too lazy to stand up and question her. One of the guards said, "They are peasants, don't bother." He signaled to the other guards who were assembled there, to give the peasants "free passage". This way the widow and the guards passed the gate unnoticed. Once she reached her street, her two guards stopped, then followed her with their eyes, until she reached her house. Soraya changed her clothes and then, properly dressed, went directly to the palace.

The palace's security men recognized her and quickly informed Zaafer Lebranki. When he heard the news, he looked at her through a small opening and then ran to the caliph, thinking he had won. He said, "My king, as I told you, our security men trapped her like a mouse, and they left only one way open to her, the way to your palace." The caliph was very happy.

"You are a genius!" answered the caliph. "I am indebted to you and congratulations on your exploit," continued the caliph. After that, both the king and Zaafer Lebranki waited patiently for her arrival.

Zaafer Lebranki, as always, used his cunning to promote himself. He gave the following instructions to his security men, "Do not let the widow approach the caliph until I give the signal to the guard standing by the door. He will convey my signal to you."

When the widow reached the caliph's quarters, she was stopped by the guard. At the same time, she noticed an old man dressed in his military uniform. His clothes were decorated with many medals, and he was walking in the same direction, to the king's door. When he saw Soraya for the first time after her return, he said, "What are you waiting for, my lady?"

Soraya did not recognize the general in his military uniform, but she recognized his eyes. She answered, "I am waiting for permission to see the caliph, Sir." The general opened the door, purposely left it wide open, and

signaled her to step in. The widow entered the king's room. The guard was stunned and embarrassed; he was caught between Zaafer Lebranki's instructions and the general's action. Zaafer Lebranki was shocked to see the widow in the room before he had had a chance to talk to the caliph and to extract from him a favor for himself, for his so-called marvelous strategy.

"Where are you going, my lady? Have you not learned to behave yourself?" said Zaafer Lebranki, but it was too late.

The general greeted the caliph, then said to Zaafer Lebranki, "Why have you left the lady waiting? I believe that the caliph has been waiting for her for a few weeks, is that not right?" But Zaafer Lebranki did not know what to answer; he was paralyzed, he couldn't do anything. The general has held him with his eyes. Zaafer Lebranki was already trembling when he heard the voice of General Omar.

The caliph's face lit up when he saw the widow. Then he said with a majestic voice, "The general is right! What are you waiting for, my lady?" The caliph was smiling and looked very happy, then he continued, "Please come in, come in!"

Soraya was at her best. She walked towards the caliph with fervor. When he saw this situation, the guard, rather frightened, gently closed the door behind her. Meanwhile Soraya, who had never seen the general in

uniform, understood that he was the old man she had met before. As soon as she was facing the caliph, she began, "My king, I have brought you what you asked for!"

The caliph thought that she was apologizing to him. Zaafer Lebranki had hinted to him before that she had come back empty-handed, so he looked at her with compassion and said, "I hope you will like it in our palace."

Soraya looked younger; with her nice dress she did not seem to be suffering or in need of the king's mercy. Soraya was rather happy and uplifted; she realized that the king was not properly informed about her. She looked at the general with a faint smile, then continued walking with such confidence that one could have said she felt at home. She turned to Zaafer Lebranki, then to the king, and said, "My king, let us admire the beautiful sight of your garden through the window."

Zaafer Lebranki, who did not know the full story, repeated after her with arrogance, "Yes, my king, show her the beautiful sight through your window! I am sure she will love it here."

The caliph was happy that events had finally come to this point. He smiled, but he did not join her, in order not to give her the impression that he wanted her humiliated. He was clever, for he knew that a woman without dignity cannot be a good partner. He waited a little longer before moving, although he wanted very much to show her the

beautiful green trees in his garden. He had the feeling he would be grabbing something that he did not deserve. Then, at the insistence of Zaafer Lebranki, he finally moved towards the window. The general did not move from his place, neither did Zaafer Lebranki. When he saw the sea of camels covering the entire street and the palace garden, the king was first shocked. Then he looked at Zaafer Lebranki with astonishment and fury and said, "You fool, you fool!" The king could not believe his eyes, and then he turned to Soraya, and with a calm and caring tone, he said, "My dear lady, are these your camels?"

The widow responded gently, "My king, is this not what you asked for?" Then she repeated the sentence that the king had used when she had pleaded with him, "'Just bring me one thousand and one female camels, all one year old and in every existing color.' These are your camels, my king! Here they are! You are now the richest camel owner in the world. Free my son!"

The caliph responded with dignity and decency. In fact, he was happy that she had succeeded, but he did not want to lose her, so he said, "No, my lady, you deserve much more than that. From now on, I declare you to be my sister! And you will enjoy all the privileges of the Persian Empire accorded to a princess. Your son is in his quarters next to my daughter Khayet, and I hope he will forgive me for the injustice we have done to him."

Soraya would not be comforted until she could see her son. She responded, "My king, now can I see my son?"

The king reacted happily and quickly, "He is the guest of my daughter, Princess Khayet."

Soraya was pleased to know that her son was not in prison. She said, "I thank our king for freeing my son from prison."

The king directed his hand toward the general and said, "This was the general's advice." Then he introduced the widow to the general.

When the latter approached Soraya, her face blushed; she acted as if she had never met him before and thanked him for his kind advice. "My son will surely thank you for what you have done for him, and of course His Majesty too, who had the wisdom to listen to your just advice."

Meanwhile, Colonel Rabiya managed to bring in the camels from many directions. The guards stood helpless as hundreds of camels entered each gate. Their security chief did not tell them what to do in such an event, as they never believed that Soraya would succeed in assembling such a huge number of camels. Zaafer Lebranki too had not had the foresight to imagine that such a situation could even occur.

Slowly, the herd penetrated almost every place and finally reached the palace courtyard, invading every free

space available around the king's palace. When he saw this unbelievable scene, Zaafer Lebranki excused himself with a false pretext and disappeared from the caliphate, leaving behind him his lovely daughter from his divorced wife.

The name of Zaafer Lebranki's daughter was Naziha, and she lived with her father in a wing of the palace. Her father knew that this time, if Soraya returned with the thousand and one camels as demanded from her by the king, he would be risking his life, as this rude judgment had been his advice. He knew that if he stayed in the palace he could be at the mercy of the king. He decided to leave the palace, but before that he would summon his closest friend in security. He had a very serious conversation with him. The security guard, who knew the ruler of the neighboring country, arranged for Zaafer Lebranki and for himself safe harbor with the Barmakid family, which had a huge house not far from Arabia. The secretary secretly kept contact with his daughter Naziha. He first communicated with her through a family member who traveled between Arabia and the Caliphate of Baghdad, but this became increasingly more dangerous, as General Omar kept a close eye on her. Eventually Zaafer Lebranki distanced himself from his daughter, so as not to put her good life at risk. After that, no one heard from him again.

General Omar had once more saved the king from a shady adventure. His influence in the palace grew stronger, and the caliph relied on him more than anyone in the palace. And this is how General Omar became the mastermind for spreading the Islamic religion.

Chapter 10

The Sisters

That day the widow took her son and went home to share the great adventure she had had with her son and her sister. The king graciously put a carriage at her disposal and told her that he was giving a party in her honor, at which she would be officially promoted to the rank of princess of the empire.

The widow did not react to the king's invitation; she hesitated for a moment, then made a sign with her head and her hand, giving the king to understand that she would think about it after she had rested. Before leaving the palace, the general gave instructions to an officer to accompany Soraya and to show the coachman the way through the city, which was crowded with one thousand and one camels and their drivers. While she was in the carriage, she had an interesting thought. *It is not so bad to be a princess,* she murmured, while her son looked at her face, as if he understood what she was thinking.

"Mother, what did the king mean by saying 'will be officially promoted to the rank of princess?'"

Soraya knew very well that her son was smart and that he must have figured out what the king wanted from her. So as not to give her son a false impression, she jumped in and said, "The king asked for my hand in marriage, and I refused."

Rahman, who was eager to know the truth, said spontaneously, "Mother, what does he mean by saying 'princess', if you refused his offer?"

Soraya was glad to answer all her son's questions, as she was prepared to tell him all about what had happened to her, but when she reached the gate of the palace, she stopped for a moment and she responded calmly, "I will tell you all about it when we arrive at home." She made a sign with her eyes towards the coachman and Rahman understood quickly that everything that was discussed in the carriage could well reach the king's ears.

Soraya turned to him and said plaintively, "I hope that this afternoon will be perfect."

Rahman smiled and asked another question which had nothing to do with anything, "Mother, do you think we have food in our house?"

Suddenly the coachman said, "If you want me to go somewhere to shop, just let me know!"

Soraya made another hint to her son and said, "No, my sister is home and she usually has everything in the house for the entire week." When they reached their

house, Soraya was sure that the coachman and the officer who accompanied them were listening to their conversation.

"Thank God, we are here!" said Rahman, smiling and looking at his mother with a silent gesture. Then he whispered to himself, *I wish my father was alive to see Mother's courage.* Then, like a child, he ran to kiss his aunt who was in the kitchen and did not hear the noise of their arrival.

When she saw him, she asked anxiously, "Have you seen your mother?"

Rahman understood that his aunt was frightened, not knowing what happened to her sister and to Rahman. He reacted quickly, "Mother, come here!" Soraya was unloading all kinds of presents that the king had put in her carriage as a surprise. She thanked the officer in charge for the expert way in which he directed the coach. After the coach and the officer had left, the two sisters and Rahman sat together. Soraya shared with them all that she had had to endure.

Then came the turn of Rahman, who during this entire period had been isolated in the palace. But he seemed healthy and was not upset about this misadventure. Soraya interjected once in a while to fill in the missing pieces of information.

After mother and son had related their different stories, the aunt relaxed and said, "After all, your adventure was not so bad," thinking of this picture of anger, emotion, and triumph. "If Soraya is to be a princess, what will happen with me?" Then, clever as she was, a spark of light suddenly seemed to come out of her.

Soraya never forgot that her sister was the one who advised her when she was young, and it had been thanks to her that she had married the husband she loved. Then Soraya with her shiny eyes jumped at her with a faint smile and said, "Now what do you have in mind?"

Leila didn't let her wait for an answer and said, "The king will pay. Between us we should not forget that we are first Arab and not Persian, and we should draw up a good plan together." Then she turned toward Soraya and said, "Did I give you good advice?" Then Soraya made a faint sign with one eye. Leila understood that she should not say anything, as Rahman was with them.

In the evening the two sisters were together, and as Leila came to give advice to Soraya she stopped her short and said, "No Leila, this time I will shape my own life myself."

Leila seemed unhappy with her sister's answer and said, "You want to marry the king? And have a good time as a queen?"

Soraya, who had acquired more experience from her recent adventure, responded, "Not at all. I will take full benefit from the king without becoming the queen."

At this juncture Leila jumped at her sister with an exclamation, "You want to live with the king as his mistress?"

Soraya looked at her sister, then paused and said in a serious tone, "Leila, I didn't mean to offend you, but there are many other honest ways to deal with a king in love. Soraya knew all along that her sister had been brought up with these feelings. Soraya was an example; she always found decent and honest ways, even if someone hurt her as the king and Zaafer Lebranki had done. She had a way of doing things, and she had been lucky to encounter men like the general and Bousid. She turned towards Leila and said, "Don't forget what our father taught us."

Then Leila repeated their father's saying, "If a lie can help, the truth can save you."

Soraya smiled at her sister and said, "Yes my dear, I could get what I wanted from the king, but I remembered our father's saying, and then I felt at peace with myself. After all, I received one thousand and one female camels." When she spoke these last words, Leila, who was annoyed by the success of her sister, continued by saying, "One year old and in every existing color." Then

both sisters smiled as they used to, and they were both happy after all.

The next day, Rahman, who did not follow the entire event, asked his mother, "What has happened to this enormous herd?" Soraya explained to him that after taking in the events of the day before, the caliph had asked the general if he could arrange for the return of the herd to its legitimate owners. Then General Omar asked the colonel to find out who was the owner of this herd and to return the huge number of camels. The king did not realize what one thousand and one camels represented. He too had never seen such a herd. The colonel was again happy to perform another task for the general. He felt that he had again the privilege to command all the guards and the camel drivers. He left the same day in a south westerly direction. But this time, in order to reach Bousid's village, he took a different route. He had to make the journey with the guards. He felt the absence of Soraya's company. He was sorry that he did not have the chance to say goodbye to her. But he was hoping to find her in the palace when he had completed his mission. By the time he reached the outskirts of Baghdad, he was convinced that Soraya would wait for him before going her way. He was busy moving the camels from one side to the other in order to lead them where he wanted. Only when he reached the river could he relax and think about her and about the entire journey. After all, he too was tired, but the fact that

a beautiful lady like Soraya had been entrusted to his protection gave him and his guards a lot of strength and enthusiasm. As a soldier he had never considered this sudden pleasant feeling. He thought that if the army had women in its ranks, the men would do the impossible just to show their power and leadership.

The first morning Soraya woke up in her house, she had the feeling that she was still moving with the herd. She ran to the window to see where she was, and she realized that the landscape was of a city and not of a village. She quickly returned to her bed, where she spent most of the morning surrounded by her usual pillows. She could hardly comprehend how she had made that trip to Bousid's and how the general had made her famous. Bousid had made a great impression on her. *This kind of person is rare in this world,* she said to herself.

While she was daydreaming about the camels and young Mokhtar, her sister entered her room and said, "Soraya, I hope you appreciate being home!"

Soraya, interrupted in her privacy, made a face and said, "Don't you see how I am enjoying being home?" Meanwhile Leila came back with a tray of tea, bread, butter, and eggs.

Soraya was very happy that her sister was taking care of her and said to her, "When I am officially a princess, I will promote you to be my first assistant."

Chapter 11

Soraya Officially Becomes a Princess

Ever since her husband's death, Soraya hadn't had a chance to wear her elegant dresses. A party offered her and her sister the opportunity to display their beauty and their charm. Rahman too was well dressed. Khayet didn't stop watching him. When the king appeared, he was stunned to see Soraya with such a beautiful dress and was amazed to see her older sister, who looked even nicer than her. This grand reception in Soraya's honor was well publicized among all the king's friends and family.

The great hall was full of neighboring kings, queens and dignitaries. When her husband was alive, Soraya had the dress made by a famous dressmaker, well known in the entire Mediterranean region. Everyone was looking at her and at her sister with great admiration. Everyone was eager to make Soraya's and her sister's acquaintance; they were also confused, as they thought that one of the two would probably be the next queen.

Then, when everyone was present, the king's voice silenced the audience as he proclaimed with

magnanimity that henceforth Soraya would be a Princess of the Kingdom. He gave her an entire region in the north of the empire as her domain and said to her, "My lady Soraya, this is your kingdom, as a present from your king."

Now it was up to Soraya to proclaim whatever she desired. She was so happy about the outcome of the entire episode that, after the king had spoken, she exchanged a few words with him and with her sister, and said, "God bless our king, the generous one and the charitable one, the king of kings, who knew how to judge right from wrong." As she said "the king of kings" all the dignitaries stood up and applauded. Leila, her sister, was thrilled to mingle with such dignitaries. When she was married, her husband had been wealthy but not well educated, and she missed cultured society. Then Soraya, who was talking with the king, smiled to all present and said, "My son, my sister and I thank our king very much for his magnificent present." Then she briefly spoke again with the king and continued, "I hereby proclaim the region that the king has chosen and offered to me to be called the Kingdom of Farhastan (Country of Happiness), and its capital will be called Farhabad (Place of Happiness), in honor of our beloved late Queen Farha. This kingdom will be an integral part of the Caliphate Empire.

As she finished her speech, the king came to the stage and added, "Princess Soraya, I congratulate you on the name you have given to one of the best regions of the Muslim Empire, but you forgot one thing." Soraya was surprised, as she didn't know what she could have forgotten. While she looked at her sister, the caliph said, "I, Harun Al-Rashid, son of the third Abassid caliph, Al-Mahdi, king of Persia and caliph of Baghdad have the honor and the power in the name of the kingdom to elevate Princess Soraya to be the queen of the Kingdom of Farhastan, which is situated on the Caspian Sea."

Then Soraya took the stage and said, "Your Majesty, I accept the noble title with pleasure, and I feel honored to bear this powerful title of the kingdom that you have just given to me. As a queen, I hope to welcome you as the most honored guest in the city of Farhabad at a time of your choosing."

The ceremony lasted till the evening, as the crowning strictly followed all the traditional Muslim rules. Harun Al-Rashid had brought the qadi (religious judge) and the Ten Leaders of the Koran. When Soraya saw the religious people, she was a little nervous, as she thought that Harun Al-Rashid might have misunderstood her; he might have thought that she had accepted to marry him. She was embarrassed, as she thought too that he might have been misled by her words and by her cheerful

161

attitude. She took her sister Leila aside to tell her about her concern.

But Leila, who listened to what she was saying, reassured her that she should not worry, as she had spoken with the king several times, and he seemed to be well aware that Soraya would not be his wife. Then she added, "He even told me that he was happy to have two sisters like us." Then Leila continued, "Do you know why he brought the religious people as witnesses? It is to have their blessing." Then she continued, "It is the custom of all kings and queens to have religious people on their side as witnesses. Christians do the same; they bring the high priest and all other ranks of priests to give to their ceremony a stamp of legitimacy." Soraya, who knew her sister very well, felt comforted and seemed confident that the king had nothing of this nature in his thoughts.

Soraya was happy and reassured and conducted herself with charm and dignity until the end of the ceremony. The king spent a lot of time with Leila too, and seemed to be satisfied with his decision. General Omar was sitting next to several foreign military attachés, but nothing that went on around him in the great hall escaped his attention. He spoke many times with Rahman and with Leila; he knew the entire story of Soraya's family.

Princess Khayet, who also looked very elegant in her dress, was cheerful and moved from one circle to another. She entertained the foreign princesses and dignitaries. Leila and the princess became close, and they spent most of the ceremony talking about her father. Khayet, who lived alone in her quarters, felt isolated most of the time. Now she was very happy to find people like Soraya, Leila and surely Rahman, for whom she had special feelings.

As the ceremony was being performed, Khayet saw herself next to Rahman, and dreamed for the rest of the day that he would be sworn in to become a king. The thought that Rahman would replace her father didn't bother her, but she also imagined a time when she could see her old father visiting her often and having more time to share with her. She also saw her father sitting next to Soraya and sharing their story as brother and sister. In fact, a few years later, the king, who was always eager to talk with Soraya and her sister, eventually built a summer castle for himself, not far from Soraya's palace, and he spent a few months every year in that lovely country of Farhastan.

General Omar, who observed all the guests during the ceremony, saw the king in a good mood when he was speaking with Leila. In fact she was even nicer than her sister Soraya and was not bound by any vow. This led him to the idea of a match for the king, to prevent him

from plunging again into depression. He used the opportunity to chat with Leila for a while. The general was happy talking with her and, when she said that her sister was lucky to be a princess, he interrupted her by saying, "How about making you a princess too?"

Leila looked at him with surprise and with an ironic smile she said, "General, with my greatest respect to you and your noble family, I don't think that it is in your power to do this."

The general looked at her with a very serious expression and said, "You may be right."

Leila, knowing what he had done for her sister, felt that she might have made a mistake by answering in this way. She started on another subject, so as not to draw attention on what she had said before. "General, I heard that your son Bousid is a very nice man. I hope that we will have an opportunity to see him."

General Omar, who understood that Leila's words were only meant to divert his attention from what she had said before, smiled and said, "How nice of you to ask about my son Bousid; he is the best son I have from my first wife. As she was very religious, she stayed in Arabia where all her family lives, and she is no longer young, as you can imagine. I married her because my family gave their word to her father, without asking for my opinion. At that time, I was too young to say no to my father, and it was customary that the parents decide whom the

children should marry. My second wife is much younger, and she is also from Arabia.

Leila smiled and said, "I know very well what you are saying. I made the same mistake by accepting the man my father wanted me to marry, and the poor man died after a short period of time." Leila started to think that maybe the general had some idea in mind and asked him, "General, if I may ask...."

General Omar was listening to her with great attention and curiosity and said, "Go ahead."

Leila made a face as though she was shy and continued politely, "Is your second wife in Baghdad?"

The general looked at her and said, "No Leila, she went with her sister, who is married to a gentleman, and she lives in Damascus."

Leila, who felt that she had moved the general's attention away from what she had earlier said, changed the subject again and told him, "If it had been me, I would not have refused the hand of a king like Harun Al-Rashid."

The general, an old fox, understood well that Leila had taken a step back, and with a slight hint he said, "He is the best king we ever had; I feel sorry that he lost his second wife Farha."

Leila, so as to show interest in what he was saying, asked, "Her name was Farha?" Then she continued, "She must have been a beautiful woman."

The general answered with regret, "She was smart and she was a happy lady, and most importantly, she was from an Arab family.

Leila saw the seriousness in his face when he said "from an Arab family." She said, "Was she a princess when she married him?"

The general didn't answer this question and went on, "It is a great loss for the king and for all of us. I counted a lot on her, but we hope to find another lady from an Arab family." Leila understood now what the general had meant when he had said, "I can make you a princess."

The idea of becoming the king's next wife pleased her very much. She murmured and faintly laughed and said, "I hope that the king will find someone from Arabia, like us." The general smiled as he understood the message that Leila would not object, like her sister, if the king asked for her hand. As soon as the guests left the ceremonial hall, the general went to the king to congratulate him on his generous performance.

Then he took leave from the king and was about to walk towards the door when the king called him,

"General, as everyone has left, and only you and I are in this room, how do you find Soraya's sister?"

The general, who had been mulling over this thought since the beginning of the ceremony, made a step back toward the king and said, "With all respect, Majesty, I found her almost as desirable as her sister Soraya."

The king seemed pleased with the general's answer and said, "I thank you for all you have done for the empire and for me." Then he left and went to his room. The general, who knew him better than anyone, was happy to receive such a response from the king and was assured of the king's intention. He went home with the hope that he would have a chance to pursue the discussion with Leila on this subject.

Chapter 12

Farhastan

For a while, the caliph of Baghdad, Rahman, Leila and Soraya, moved to her new castle in Farhastan, in the north of the empire. The caliph realized that Soraya was an honest and decent lady; he never knew that she was of pure Arabian origin, and a good Muslim, and since he considered her now as his own sister, he often sought her advice. He felt that he couldn't have found better family members than her and her sister. As he became less and less interested in state affairs, he eventually retained Rahman as his secretary of state, who dealt with daily business. General Omar was very happy to see the developments taking shape in the direction he had intended and was watching the progress from his office. In fact Leila thanked the general for having arranged her marriage with the king. Even if it had not been her dream initially, but after years as a widow, being married to a king was a great honor.

Rahman became the most trusted man in the palace, and later the king voluntarily designated him to be his

successor. Rahman, who was already a close friend of princess Khayet's, Harun Al-Rashid's only daughter, didn't know any other young girl and became attached to her. After years in the palace, he learned the art of governing. His job took his entire time. Khayet, who had more time than he did, was bored in her quarters.

One day she asked Rahman to come to her, as she had something urgent to discuss with him. Rahman, who was very busy, as he took his job seriously, never divulged his feelings to her, but he loved her very much. Khayet was similar to her mother, she was bright and cheerful, and as Rahman could not resist her charm, he answered her request immediately. He rushed to her quarters, believing that something had happened to her. When he reached her room, Khayet was lying on her sofa. When she saw him, she smiled and waved her hand as a sign for him to come closer. Rahman was frightened to see her lying down; this seemed strange to him; until then, although she was always in a good mood, she had always been well behaved. When he approached her sofa, she gave him her hand, and as he held her hand, Khayet unexpectedly pulled him to her. Rahman, who was educated all his life to observe the decencies, fell on her. He was confounded and didn't know what to say. Khayet, who had planned this scenario, laughed and kept holding his hand. Rahman stood up and apologized for this incident. Khayet kept laughing. Rahman finally asked her why she had called. Khayet kept laughing, as

though nothing had happened, and didn't answer his question. When Rahman was ready to walk out, Khayet asked him, "You don't want to see me?"

Rahman, ashamed of himself and all confused, answered apologetically, "No, no . . . yes, of course!"

Khayet, who was relaxed, continued to laugh and said, "Sit next to me on the sofa!" Rahman, who in fact was eager to have her, sat next to her but discreetly kept his distance, as he wanted to appear well behaved. Khayet, who didn't want to push him too much, understood that in his position he owed her respect. She stood up, then asked him, "Would you like a cup of tea?"

Rahman felt uncomfortable and responded absentmindedly, "Yes, of course!" Khayet smiled, as she was satisfied with his gentle behavior, and ordered the servant to bring two cups of tea and some pastries. Both spent the afternoon enjoying their conversation. This encounter didn't escape General Omar, who had many servants spying for him. He was happy with this outcome. The next day he visited Rahman and advised him to marry Khayet. Rahman trusted the general, as he knew that he was the man who had saved his mother from the king's impossible demand. Taking into consideration that the general had unshackled him from the darkness of the jail, Rahman was overwhelmed with the happy development and gladly accepted General

Omar's proposal to marry Princess Khayet, thereby keeping the power in the family.

Soraya had permanently moved to her new castle in the north of the empire, Farhastan. The general, who was now the only worthy and loyal man of the king, had replaced Zaafer Lebranki. He died a few years later from pneumonia. Eventually, the caliph retired to his northern palace, which was under Queen Soraya's jurisdiction.

Soraya knew how to attract the respect of many kings and heads of neighboring countries. She organized all kinds of activities and festivities, which became a major source of revenue to the country and to the palace. She was admired for her beauty and her charm and foremost for her religious devotion.

The economy of Farhastan was booming, and her treasury grew tremendously from princes and kings who sent her presents in gold and precious stones. The Kingdom of Farhastan was at peace. Colonel Rabiya, who became the defense secretary of Farhastan, never had to prove himself a good soldier. Everyone in the region knew him because of General Omar's recommendation and his past battle against the Byzantines. Soraya knew how to keep peace with all the surrounding countries. She took the example of King Solomon who never fought a war in his entire reign. She made treaties with many countries; the kings and the

princes considered her to be their best ally. Her palace was open almost daily to guests who came to visit her.

Colonel Rabiya could not have had a better life. He was constantly invited to many countries and enjoyed tremendous admiration from the princesses. He was smart and knew how to please the princesses without committing himself to anyone. Soraya's son, Rahman, was well received in general. The king, who liked him too, made him the caliph of Baghdad. He fulfilled his function as caliph very well. Since he had taken on this job, he had elevated the prestige of the king. Harun Al-Rashid never took a decision without getting advice and input from Rahman.

Leila became the queen but she never did anything for the king or the empire. The king was finally happy to be with Leila and this way he became an integral member of Soraya's family. Harun Al-Rashid spent his time between his daughter Khayet and Leila. The latter was the only one who knew how to deal with him and how to entertain him. Soraya, who was very religious, was cheerful, although she kept a certain distance. Finally, the king realized that Leila was in fact better for him than Soraya. Rahman became a very wise and good king. He too enjoyed great respect like his mother, and every king wanted to have him as a friend. Harun Al-Rashid's kingdom prospered and enjoyed a stability never known before.

*

Let us now return to Bousid, his son Mokhtar, and colonel Rabiya.

The general had told Rabiya that he had to return the camels to his son Bousid. After enduring a few exhausting days, Rabiya reached Bousid's village. He decided to keep the herd in an open field and passed on the responsibility to Bousid. Some of the camels were left grazing in Bousid's pasture, waiting for his son Mokhtar to return from the south and from Arabia, where he spent over a month on his trip returning the larger number of camels. Then Bousid gave his son, who was already tired from his long trip, the second mission, to return the rest of camels to their legitimate owners in the surrounding area. Many owners were friends and family members. As they had previously spent a lot of time recording the account of everyone who had lent them camels, it was easy to recognize which were whose camels, as they had marked with color the identity of the owner on each camel. Mokhtar's uncle and Bousid's friends had given the largest number of camels. Mokhtar had listened to his father's advice to visit an aunt. He spent some time there.

There he made the acquaintance of a nice young girl, and when he returned home, he told his father about her. Later he married this young lady with the blessing of his father. Her name was Aziza. Three years had passed and

Aziza had not given him a child. Aziza spent her time riding on her horse with the guards and going back and forth to her parents. Her behavior was unacceptable in the Arab world. And to add to it, she wasted a lot of good money from Bousid's estate. Bousid did not like her from the beginning, as he found her to be vulgar. She did not care about the house, and when she was home she wasted her time gazing out of her window.

Bousid did not say a word, as she was new in their house. The wedding alone had cost Bousid a fortune. He had to pay her father the equivalent value of five hundred horses. Although she was a Muslim, she was not of pure Arabian origin. At that time, Bousid did not object to his son marrying her. Out of love and respect for him, Bousid did not bargain at all with Aziza's father, as was the custom at that time. The happiness of his son meant much more to him than any material value. Mokhtar had proven to his father that he was a generous and loyal son.

Bousid returned to his usual daily work. He helped many villagers to get on their feet. He used to say that neighbors should be helped and should never be left without anything. He was proud that no one starved in his village. He took care of all the widows and the orphans. They all lived from farming the field that Bousid had given to them. He was like their father and their tribal chief. He was loved and respected in the entire region for his generosity and for his wisdom.

175

If any dispute arose in the village, Bousid was the only one who could settle the matter. Bousid knew how to make two adversaries friends. As soon as the dispute arose, he brought the two parties to work with him in the field. This way he could observe them, and the two parties had to talk and work together. By the end of the day their differences would become irrelevant. In many cases, the parties became friends after being with one another for a few days or a week. It was up to Bousid to determine the time he kept them on the job. Those who worked with him received a good salary for their work. Everyone found his rulings fair, as no one was either a winner or a loser.

Bousid was happy that this entire operation was completed and he hadn't lost anything. He regretted that his wife was stingy and lacking confidence. He said to Mokhtar, "Life is what we do with it. God was generous with us and gave us the entire fortune. Why should we be less generous? As colonel Rabiya has returned all the camels, he is clearly a good and trustworthy man, and he should stay with us and enjoy the place." When he saw him, he invited him to stay at least for a while to relax and enjoy the fresh air and good milk and butter.

The colonel didn't rush to go back. He enjoyed the area, and he felt at home at Bousid's place. He had the use of a good horse during his stay. In order to let his horse enjoy the vast prairie and the rich grass, Rabiya

176

liked to roam in the area and especially to go back to the fortress. He used to stay for hours and remember how he had captured this stronghold from the Byzantine soldiers. He considered Bousid as his brother, as he had spent many days in his house before. Bousid too liked Rabiya. He was the most trusted man in his family. Bousid gave him a letter to his father, General Omar, in which he said that Rabiya was even better than a member of their family.

Afterwards Rabiya returned to the palace, gave his report to General Omar and went home. During his absence, Soraya had asked the general if she could have the colonel as her defense secretary. General Omar, without saying anything, found this request to be very good for his general scheme. He advised Rabiya to take the job offered to him by Soraya, as the head of the defense of her Kingdom of Farhastan. He told him that many opportunities would present themselves in the future.

When the Kingdom of Farhastan was created, Rabiya, who wanted badly to be with Soraya, whom he found very pleasant to work with, became her chief of staff and the head of security. He spent his time anticipating imaginary attacks from the neighboring countries, which even the caliph feared the most. He respected Queen Soraya after their journey to Bousid's house. His experience and his knowledge gained him respect.

Soraya was not prepared to take him as a husband, and their relations were based on dignity and honor. Although he was Muslim, he was not of pure Arabian origin, but a pure Persian. He could not joke with Soraya, as their relations were respectful and serious. He never knew that Soraya secretly wanted him, and she would have married him if he had been of pure Arabian origin. He spent his time as an unmarried man waiting for a new battle, which never came. Soraya had kept her vow to her husband. She couldn't get married again and, as a queen, she felt obligated to her son, the caliph, to General Omar and to all those who knew her. She remained a widow.

Chapter 13

Bousid

Times go and times come. Soraya never knew what became of Bousid El Hallali and his generous son Mokhtar. Meanwhile, years and years passed; our friend Bousid became old, and his son never recovered from his divorce. Mokhtar's wife appeared from time to time in his village. Her sudden presence was unbearable for Mokhtar and his father. She was challenging their honor. Finally Bousid intervened and told his son to settle with her with money. Mokhtar paid her a huge sum of money just to get rid of her and to have peace of mind. After the death of General Omar, Bousid was left in disarray. His estate was impoverished by the raids of Zaafer Lebranki's security men, who were still loyal to their former boss. They were secretly directed by Zaafer Lebranki to avenge him by punishing the son of General Omar. In fact he succeeded in destroying the entire assets of the Bousid family. They took his entire fortune, as they knew that General Omar was no longer alive to defend their honor or their goods. Finally Bousid was left without a house or any material possession. But Zaafer

Lebranki's security men left him with a few donkeys, so that he and his son could make a living by the sweat of their brow. Bousid didn't lose faith and he always said, "Everything is from Allah." With his donkeys he could do something. Meanwhile Al-Rashid, who gave his throne to Rahman, who married his daughter, grew old and no longer had any interest in his empire. Bousid became a small ceramic merchant and sold his pots from town to town and from village to village. All the pottery makers, who for the most part were women, knew him very well from the time he had been rich and generous. They were all upset about the king and Zaafer Lebranki, as Bousid had helped many of them in bad times. He enjoyed great respect from these women, and he received hospitality everywhere. The entire region knew him and had known his late father.

After many years, he finally ventured to go to the Kingdom of Farhastan. He was eighty years old and traveled with a few donkeys and a few young boys from the villages that supplied him with pottery. He concluded a deal with those women who needed him, as at that time women could not travel alone. The deal he had made with these women was that every ceramic crafter would give a donkey loaded with pottery and a young boy to help him move these goods north. It was known to everyone that Farhastan was a rich country and that everyone who came from there bragged about the sales he made in that country. Bousid was not the only one

who was attracted to this area. Along with the pottery, he even took some fine rugs to sell. In fact it was like a consignment arrangement, which was customary in that region. No one had much capital with which to buy and sell goods.

It took almost a month for Bousid and his caravan to reach the capital of Farhastan, which was known in that region as Farhabad. The crossing of the desert and the various rivers was not so difficult, as the boys were used to the climate and to the terrain. The desert was sometimes stony and sometimes sandy. After the desert, they had to climb many slopes with the donkeys. The Persian side was mountainous and sometimes rocky. The animals were exhausted, as they carried voluminous and heavy loads of merchandise, and the sand was so thin that their hoofs sank in the sand, making it hard for them to move forward. Bousid had to stop many times, as the young boys too were tired and had to rest once in a while. The caravan stopped at night to eat and relax. From time to time they had to rearrange the loads, as the pottery was very fragile. Bousid showed the young boys how to attach the loads to avoid any damage. When they had to cross water, a smart young boy had an idea: he attached the bundles in a long line, swam to the other side with a rope, and then he pulled all the cargo across. Bousid felt very responsible for the women, as he had known them all for years. He was like a father to them. When their husbands were alive, they had worked for him. Farhabad

was situated near the western shore of the Caspian Sea and extended toward the north and the south. Many visitors came from the north by ship and by boat. Bousid moved his donkeys over hard terrain. When he reached Farhabad he was tired and so were the youths. He stopped next to a large tree to relax under its shade.

The security services of Farhabad were informed of the new vendor and, as he had to have a permit authorizing him to sell goods from other areas, they intercepted him. Bousid had never needed any permit and, particularly when his father, General Omar, was in charge, he had enjoyed many privileges owing to his father's position. When the security guards saw the beautiful rugs and the ceramics, they invited him to come to the palace to sell his goods there. Bousid was happy with this invitation. He had not been in any palace since the days of General Omar. He had the feeling that if he met the queen, something good would come out of it. After all, the queen must have enough money to buy beautiful pottery such as he was carrying.

When the security guards and his caravan reached the palace, the queen was watching through her window. She was curious to see who these people were. She waited until the caravan reached a position where she could clearly distinguish the faces of the vendors, and she had the feeling that the old vendor resembled old Bousid. She asked the security guards to identify him. When they

came back with his name, she recognized old Bousid. She remembered that she was greatly indebted to him. She couldn't understand why this generous and rich man was with a caravan of donkeys. Then she wondered why she hadn't seen him at the funeral of his father, General Omar. She had wanted to see him for a long time.

Bousid was tired and old, but his features had not changed. Without knowing the reason, she felt sorry for this man. Now that he was in her town and under her jurisdiction, she wanted to prepare a great surprise for him. In fact, since the days when she went to him, she had trusted only the Omar family and the colonel. She had a plan for receiving Bousid, and after thinking for a while she came up with an idea of a scenario in two parts. First she had to create a dramatic scene to push him to his emotional limits, and then she would receive him like a king. For the emotional part she would send a dozen of young ladies from her entourage to look at the pottery and then to say, each after the other, "Oh, my God, this is beautiful" and, as if by accident, break all his pottery, one piece at a time. The poor man would have no other choice than to seek justice. He would have to come to her with a complaint.

The girls acted according to the queen's plan. Poor Bousid found himself embroiled in a dispute that was not to his liking. He had never experienced anything like this. It was painful for the old man, especially after such

a hard trip, to see his merchandise, which belonged to the widows, broken in pieces. He demanded of the security guards to see the head of the authority of this town. The guards told him to go see Queen Soraya. The name did not ring a bell with poor Bousid. He was too tired, and too many years had passed for him to remember a name. He didn't know what was happening to him. He prepared to see the queen and to complain to her, when a guard came toward him and told him he could not see the queen with such clothes and that he should take a bath beforehand. Bousid smiled and said, "I have no objection to a bath, but I am not in my city nor in my house."

The guard, who was prepared in advance, responded spontaneously, "It is all right, you can take a bath in the guards' quarters, which are located in the palace", and he directed him to another man who was already waiting to accompany him to the bath chamber. When he was in the bath, Bousid thought that he was dreaming, as there were many ladies waiting to help him. The barber was there too, to cut his hair and shave him. The ladies were holding Chinese fans in their hands, and were saying, "God protect our sir!" (Allah Yonsor Sidna.)

Bousid interrupted them and said, "Just a minute, you are mistaking me for another gentleman. I am a poor ceramic vendor and not a noble man." But the girls didn't listen to him and kept saying the same thing over and over again. Finally Bousid saw that no one was paying

any attention to him and he let the barber do his job, and the masseur took care of his old body.

The ladies, wearing new and elegant dresses, kept repeating these words, "God protect our sir."

Bousid was certain that he was mistaken for another man and did not want to be blamed for it. He kept repeating, "I am not a nobleman; I am a poor ceramic merchant." Once he was dressed, a man accompanied him to the queen's quarters, where he had to wait for someone to receive him.

Then a well-dressed lady came through another door and told him, "Will you please follow me?"

Bousid was quite troubled and didn't know where the lady was leading him. He followed her from hallway to hallway, from spacious room to spacious room. As he walked and walked, he was frightened that he would not be able to find his way out. He interrupted the lady and said, "My lady, I believe that you are leading a stranger; I am not even from this area. I am from the village of Hallali, which is located on the Syrian frontier."

The lady hardly turned her head and said, "We know all about you; just follow me please."

Bousid was dressed like a king and after so many days of travel, he didn't care anymore about any punishment. After all, he was clean and well dressed and by following the lady, he had nothing to lose. When they reached a

magnificent large room, he caught a glimpse of a beautiful woman sitting on the queen's throne. Bousid didn't recognize her and again said, "Your Highness…. My lady, they are mistaken. I am a poor pottery merchant from far away trying to help many widows in our village, and at my age I have nothing to do. I felt that it was my duty to help them before I died."

Queen Soraya was listening to the generous and compassionate man. Meanwhile, she had invited her top staff and advisors to sit on both sides of the hall. In the middle was a red carpet and Bousid had to walk on it to approach the queen. When he reached a point where she could see him closely, he said, "Your Majesty, I am coming to you today to complain about something very small for you to judge. I intended to see a lower level authority to resolve my problem."

She addressed him in a gentle voice, "Welcome to our palace, man of dignity and great nobility!"

Bousid kept repeating, "Your Majesty, I am not the man you think I am."

Soraya, turning her head to the palace audience, said, "Do not listen to this man; he is the most humble man I have ever encountered." Bousid thought his life had come to a close this time; not only had he no money and no pottery anymore, but now he could well be accused of being a swindler. He did not know what to do; he was waiting for his sentence, and he knew that in such a case

the authorities were always right, and no one was there to defend him. He finally gave up and prayed to God for mercy.

Then, suddenly, the queen addressed him with these words, "Sidna Bousid (Sir Bousid), if I am not mistaken, you are Sidna Bousid?"

Bousid was afraid to deny his name, so he respectfully responded by saying, "Yes, Your Majesty." Then, knowing that Zaafer Lebranki and his security people were after him, he thought that they were trying to frame him, as they had done at the cost of his entire fortune. Then he said to himself, *God knows what the security people are up to this time.* He looked at the queen and said again to himself, *After all, they are everywhere, those Zaafer Lebranki security people; they are only able to injure and ruin people.* He looked at the queen again and honestly replied, "Yes, Your Majesty, you are well informed, I am the poor Bousid, without a house and without a village and now without my merchandise, because of a few uneducated ladies who broke my pottery without compassion. I came from far away to give your citizens the opportunity to buy beautiful ceramics made in Syria by honest widowed ladies. They wanted to earn their livelihood with dignity and honor. I submit my will to Your Majesty, to judge for herself and to compensate her poor servant with whatever Your Majesty deems appropriate."

Soraya listened to Bousid's argument and smiled in her heart. Then she said, "Sidna Bousid, our Almighty is big. He brought you to me. Do you remember me, the widow you so generously hosted in your house? You gave me one thousand and one female camels, one year old and in every existing color."

Bousid looked at her and said, "I never gave anything; it was our Almighty who gave it, everything belongs to Him, and as I said before, Your Majesty is taking me for someone else. I am a poor ceramic merchant. I was just trying to earn my livelihood with honor and dignity."

Soraya was very touched by Bousid's modesty. She told her story to her closest audience, and then she asked, "Where were you when General Omar passed away?"

Bousid looked at her with distress and said, "Did you know my father?"

Soraya responded, "Of course, it was he, who sent me to you."

Bousid tried to clear up some confusion but he was skeptical about the entire matter. He murmured, "I never understood what was going on that day. The moment they announced the death of my father, soldiers and people from the government came to the village and took everything from me. I was dispossessed of my house and of my land. They left me with a few donkeys, one meager ewe and one dog. My son was left with only one donkey,

188

and since then he has lost the will to work again. Do you understand, Your Majesty?" Bousid was suddenly crying with sorrow and love, since he had not told anyone about it until that day, as he never trusted government people. He answered, "Your Majesty, that was the reason why I didn't show up for the funeral."

As he was about to continue, Soraya interrupted him and said, "Sidna Bousid, from now on you will not have to fear anyone. I am Soraya, the lady you treated with compassion and with generosity."

Bousid felt like he was in a dream. He couldn't fathom what was happening to him. He thanked God for the miracle he was about to live. Then, with a gracious face, he said, "Your Majesty, I always relied on God. I have never doubted for a moment his existence deep within ourselves. I always believed that sooner or later He would show to everyone His goodness, His compassion, His strength and above all His beauty. I believed that everyone here on earth has everything within himself to find the way of God without being shackled by any religion that tries to impose on us a belief through the power of the sword. Your Majesty, I remember now the day you came to visit me in our simple village. I felt at that time that you were a messenger of the Almighty. And through my father's letter, God bless his soul, I knew that your family was noble and descendants of our prophet."

Soraya and the entire audience was listening to Bousid's words attentively and with admiration. The queen was touched by his honesty and his piety. She reflected that people like Bousid were rare in the world. Now she felt more than anytime that the love she had for her husband should be offered to Bousid. Then she said, "From now on, you will be the King of Farhastan. I have waited for a long time for this day. I thank God, who brought you here. As for your son, he will have nothing to worry about anymore. He will have the best and the most honest woman on earth. The woman I am talking about is Naziha, and she lives right here in our palace."

Bousid was moved by this noble lady, whom he had trusted from the day she appeared on his father's horse; she resembled a fairy. He felt comfortable with her, and he felt that her presence cheered up his life. He was very happy for himself and for his son Mokhtar. Soraya refrained from telling him who Naziha's father was, as she didn't want to awaken any bad feeling. Since he was already badly hurt by Zaafer Lebranki's guards, his name would antagonize him before knowing the entire story. A few days later she had the opportunity to tell him all about Naziha and her father, but Bousid was calm and showed a lot of understanding. She also told him the reason why she had waited until then to tell him about Zaafer Lebranki. He agreed with her and said, "If you had told me before, I would have burst out with anger,

because Zaafer Lebranki was probably the man behind all my misery."

Soraya knew what he meant and she showed much understanding for his plight. She told him that Zaafer Lebranki was no longer the adviser of the caliph, and that he had disappeared the day she returned with the camels and had entered the caliph's palace. He left behind his poor daughter Naziha. Then she added, "Thanks to your generous deed, I was able to return with the one thousand and one camels . . . "

"It was God's will" interjected Bousid.

But she continued, "That day, I promised his daughter Naziha, who was downhearted at the time, that she didn't have to worry and that I would find her the right husband. She listened to me, and since she has never disobeyed me, she lives with me as a princess in my palace. She has her own living quarters and has never asked for her father."

Bousid looked at her and thanked God in his heart for resolving two problems at the same time. Then Bousid bowed towards Soraya and said, "My queen, I thank you for wanting to help me and my son with your judgment."

Soraya understood that Bousid did not get the message. He seemed tired and confused, so she repeated, "My king, I submit my will to Your Majesty."

Bousid was entirely confused. He turned his head to see if the queen was talking to someone else, as he didn't grasp what she was saying. Deep in his mind he thought he heard her saying, "General Omar". He thought he was dreaming and asked the queen, "Can I go now?"

Soraya understood that this encounter was overwhelming for a man of his age. She instructed her servants to accompany him to his living quarters, hoping that after one night of good sleep he would regain his clarity and that the next day he would feel better. She thought that she would continue the conversation where she had left off. After all, she had enough time ahead of her and felt sorry that a man like Bousid had to endure so much suffering, while she was so close to the power and no one had told her about him. She sent a messenger to her son to tell him about the injustice done to Bousid and to advise him to watch his security people carefully.

When Bousid reached his living quarters, he asked the lady who was taking care of him, "What is this?"

The lady replied, "God bless our king!" Bousid was now certain that he was taken for someone else or that he was dreaming.

Then he said to the lady, "Would you please bite my finger?" The lady obeyed immediately and bit his finger. Bousid screamed to the sky so that other women working next to his quarters came running. Bousid realized that he was not dreaming, but as they kept saying, "God bless

192

our king," he murmured to himself *I should accept to be a king, especially at my old age, even for a short period of time. It would certainly be worth my while.* Then he remembered his father's saying, "It is better to live one day as a lion than a thousand days as a dog." Bousid looked again around him and continued, "If they find out that they are mistaken, I will have lived one day as a king, which is better than the life of a poor man. I have lived until now with the donkeys and the pottery."

The lady gave him his night gown and waited until he had gone to bed. Then she closed the door behind her and disappeared. A few minutes later two sweet girls came next to his bed to keep him company. Each one sat on a small stool next to his bed and waited patiently all night in the event he needed anything, such as a glass of water. Bousid was so tired and didn't move until the morning. A ray of the sun woke him up. Then, as he stood up, he saw the two girls sitting next to his bed. At first he was surprised, but then he realized that the night before he had voluntarily accepted to be a king even for a day. When he asked for his clothes, two men appeared, holding a beautiful king's gown. They saluted him with, "God bless our king!"

He saluted them in return and said, "Where is the queen of yesterday?"

They replied, "She will be here as soon as possible, my king."

Bousid liked this game and said to himself, *They wanted to make me a king for a joke? Why not? Let it be!*

Later in the morning the queen ordered that he be a judge. After all, she wanted him to be the king and, as a king, he had to judge the worse cases once a week. After his breakfast the queen arrived in his quarters and said with a charming tone, "Good morning, my king. Have you had a good night's sleep?" Bousid looked at her. He couldn't see any sign of a joke or of someone who didn't know what she was doing. The queen was serious in her behavior. She sat next to him in her elegant day dress. Bousid offered her a cup of tea. She gladly accepted, as she was now sure that he had regained his strength and that he recognized her. She took a sip of tea, then said to him, "King Bousid, son of General Omar."

He looked at her with a surprised face and with a firm voice said to her, "Do you know my father?"

"Of course!" responded Soraya."He was the one who sent me to you, and I am very grateful to you and awfully sorry for not having been able to come to your help."

Bousid looked at her over and over. He was still entirely confused. Then he looked at her with an astonished face and said, "Are you Soraya, the widow? The lady whom my father sent to me?" Soraya nodded as a sign of agreement.

"My God, my father never told me that you were a queen, but I had the feeling that you were an important person in distress."

"Correct," answered the queen. I became a queen due to your noble generosity and your understanding." Then she added, "How is your wife and your son?"

Meanwhile Bousid regained his full clarity and in a soft voice he answered, "My son is now in distress, and he lost the will to work after the government took our fortune." Bousid sighed deeply and then continued, "As for my wife, I gave her enough money for her entire life. My only concern is my son; he does not deserve to inherit my plight."

Soraya responded quickly, "What happened to you and to your son?" Then, without waiting for his answer, she added, "My king, do not worry about your son, I have already thought about him for a long time and, if you recall, I told you that I have a woman for him, who is a princess and worthy of the generosity of your son."

Bousid responded politely, "I understand your desire to do good by us, but I am happy as I am, and I will take life one day at a time. My son is not a prince and he cannot be one. I am Bousid son of General Omar."

Soraya responded with a kind smile, "Of course we know who your father is, but now you are the great man!

And you will be the king. I am a woman and tired of handling the affairs of state."

As she was talking, Colonel Rabiya entered the room and said, "King Bousid, son of General Omar, I am at your disposal as I was under your father. I am graced to serve the son of my esteemed General. You just have to let me know what I have to do."

Bousid felt much more secure when he saw the colonel. His father had told him before that he was the only man he could trust. Then Bousid said to the colonel, who meanwhile had become the secretary of defense and the chief of the entire security staff, "I want to see you in my cabinet alone." The colonel greeted Bousid as he used to greet General Omar and left the room immediately. Bousid was serious; he went straight away to his chamber. He sent everyone out. He wanted to speak with Secretary Rabiya without any witnesses.

When the colonel entered Bousid's office, the latter made him a sign to close the door behind him and asked him, "Where were you when my father died?" The colonel sighed, and then he answered, "I learned about the death of the general a few months after he was buried, and that was on the occasion of the queen's son's wedding with Princess Khayet." Bousid was listening closely to the colonel, when Rabiya suddenly burst out, "I heard that you didn't want to go to the funeral of your father as you had a lot of work."

Bousid was not shocked to hear such a lie; he knew that the government people were able to fabricate anything they wanted. He kept his calm and let the colonel continue his explanation, and then he said in a very gentle voice, "Is it safe to talk here?" The colonel answered positively. Then Bousid continued, "Do you know what happened to me and my son?"

The colonel answered firmly, "No, I was not in Baghdad! I was here on duty serving the queen on the recommendation of your father."

Then Bousid took Rabiya's hand and said, "Now, let me tell you what happened to us after my father died." The colonel, who had one day sworn to his general that he would defend the Omar family with his body if needed, reddened; his face was bursting with anger. Bousid had never known this side of the colonel.

When Bousid had finished telling his story, he said, "My king, I am loyal to you and to your family, even before your crowning, and it will be an honor for me to avenge your suffering." Then he continued, "I will lay the entire Persian Empire at your feet, if needed."

Bousid, who had never been a warrior, made a sign with his hand and said, "My first objective is to find my son and to bring him here without telling him anything about our real situation. You will tell him that you think that his father had inherited a domain from the Omar family, and that he wants him to come with you, and that

you will bring him safely to him. Then, as to revenge, a noble family will never use vengeance as a tool for any purpose whatever. Now, I will go back to the queen and you will go silently as I told you, without attracting any attention."

During the conversation the colonel had had the chance to tell him about himself and Queen Soraya. The entire episode was the scheme and the will of General Omar. Before going to Farhastan with Queen Soraya, the colonel had spent an entire night with the general. During that night the general had conveyed his thoughts about his entire plan to the colonel.

Bousid didn't waste any time. He saluted the colonel and went to the king's quarters, where Soraya was waiting for him. Bousid then put on the judge's gown and went to the court hall with Soraya.

She introduced him to the staff in the following way, "I have the pleasure and the honor of introducing to you your future king, the son of a great hero, the famous General Omar."

The staff greeted Bousid with, "God bless our king and our queen!"

The audience stood up and cheered, "God bless our king and our queen."

Bousid looked majestic, despite his age. He was well dressed and relaxed. Soraya's story was well known to

everyone, and everyone was eager for her to get married again. She was an example for her people, but after so many years since her husband had died, everyone felt that it was time for her to have a king.

Bousid listened to every case presented to him. Then he sent everyone home and adjourned all the cases till the next year, saying, "Everyone go home to your family until next year, and everyone will try to resolve his dispute without any court intervention, and if you do not manage to solve your problems between yourselves, you will come back here and it will be my duty to right the wrongs." Everyone went home and within a few months succeeded in solving their differences alone.

Chapter 14

Soraya and Bousid's Wedding

The wedding and the crowning were planned for the same month and would take place one year later, so that all the guests would be able to enjoy many events at one time and stay in the country for an entire month and even longer. The beneficial effect of a month-long wedding was calculated in the planning by Bousid and Soraya. Everyone in Farhastan would benefit from the comings and goings of the noble visitors.

Soraya was beloved by all the surrounding neighbors and even from as far away as China and Japan. Messengers on horseback worked day and night bringing messages from all over the world. All the inns were reserved in advance by every embassy in Farhabad. The construction of many new caravanserais and inns was planned, to enable the city of Farhabad to accommodate the dignitaries. Within the period preceding the wedding, and during the month of the crowning, the economy of the state had seen an enormous boom and expansion. The popularity of the queen had grown immensely. Everyone

was happy for her. Just before the wedding, Mokhtar, Bousid's son, arrived with the colonel. He was already well dressed. The secretary of defense had taken care of him. He appeared in the palace dressed like a prince. He was very handsome, and all the queen's ladies-in-waiting, who were there, admired him. Everyone wanted to capture his attention for herself, but Mokhtar didn't disappoint anyone.

Bousid was very happy to see him. Mokhtar was completely taken by surprise, and he asked his father, "Father, what is this all about?"

Bousid said to him, "Do you remember the day you went with your horse to return all the herd that I had given to a lady, as your mother instructed you? And you decided not to return the camels, and instead you added your horse on top as a sign of your approval. You were not mistaken, my son, you are worthy to be a prince; you had given your horse to a queen. Now you understand?"

Mokhtar, who hardly realized what was going on, said, "Father, when I saw that lady at that time, a sense of dignity and honor seized my entire being. I felt ashamed not to honor your donation to such a noble and gracious woman. Deep in my heart I felt that nothing would be lost. And I saw my feeling confirmed when she returned all the camels the same month."

Bousid looked at his son with admiration and said, "My dear son, nothing is lost in our lives, but we human

beings do not have the patience to wait to see the end. Now that you are relaxed and happy again, let me tell you the second piece of news. The queen has adopted and looked after Zaafer Lebranki's daughter for many years. Her father was the adviser to Harun Al-Rashid. He was the one who orchestrated our ruin. He is the man who gave bad advice to the king, so as to make Queen Soraya suffer. Since Soraya came back with the camels, which he did not expect, he saw himself exposed to the king's wrath and chose to disappear from the face of the earth. The queen wanted you to marry this young lady. She is much younger than you and she is still not married. The queen promised her a long time ago to provide her with a man worthy of her education and love."

Mokhtar interrupted his father and said, "Who is this worthy man?"

Bousid looked at him with a smile and responded, "You, Mokhtar."

"Me?"

"Yes, my son, you! Soraya couldn't find us, as she had left Baghdad to become Queen of Farhastan."

Mokhtar was taken aback. He asked his father, "Father, and what is your position?"

Bousid, "You should marry her and take care of her. You will not be disappointed again. She is very well

203

educated and obedient, and you should have children with her."

Mokhtar hugged his father and said, "I am your son, I didn't listen to your reservations about my first wife. I was wrong. I will marry her as you said, and I will have children with her. I am too tired, and I want to have a home and a family."

Father and son were about to leave the room when the colonel appeared again and said, "My king, the ambassador of India wants to see you, and I believe it is very important. You should consider granting him an immediate audience."

Bousid responded firmly and briefly, "In a moment, I first have to finish with my son! He is the Prince of Farhastan. Please wait a moment outside."

Mokhtar was overwhelmed by this entire development and said, "Father, go! It is important! I will wait here."

Bousid responded, "No, you come with me! I would like to introduce you to the ambassador." Mokhtar, who had always respected his father, was not surprised by the way his father was handling the political matter. Bousid seemed better than any king. He had with him the most precious asset, his experience.

During the meeting, the ambassador of India tried many times to impress the son of the courageous general,

but Bousid was so relaxed that the ambassador, who had come to try to convince the future king to be the closest ally of his country, in order to obtain some concessions from Caliph Rahman, the son of the old widow, and king of the Persian Empire. The ambassador was convinced that, with Farhastan as an ally, he would be in a better bargaining position. He believed that, together with Bousid, India would have better leverage to obtain some territorial concessions for areas previously taken from India. When the ambassador saw Bousid's firmness and determination, he rolled back his plan. The ambassador didn't know the relationship between Bousid and the king of Persia. Bousid, who had not yet been officially crowned, had recommended to the ambassador to tell his king to stay quiet and not to give King Rahman any excuse to conquer more territories from India, as he was now prepared for a new conquest campaign. Mokhtar had listened to the entire conversation between the ambassador and his father. Later, it became known to Bousid that the ambassador of India had recommended to his king, who was on his way to Farhastan, to forget about any concessions and to offer a large gift to the new king instead.

Already, with his first audience, Bousid had brought a fortune to the treasury. The gift from India was composed of gold, silk, and precious stones. The entire gift was prepared for another purpose. Its value could buy more than ten thousand camels.

Soraya was immediately informed about the audience and the discussion Bousid had had with the ambassador. She congratulated him and added, "I am happy to have a man with me. You succeeded better than I ever could have with my charm." She smiled and continued, "I am not surprised by your talent. I saw it the night you invited me for dinner. You managed to conquer my heart without any open word of love."

Bousid, who understood what she was hinting at, said, "Only the end counts, my lady. Now you have me for the rest of my life."

The preparations for the coronation and the wedding went on. The city of Farhabad filled up slowly, slowly with people, horses, and carriages, not to mention the fortunes and the goods every guest brought with him. The day of the wedding, the palace looked more impressive and more festive than ever. One could smell the air of joy in every corner. Bousid had set things straight, and no one could come to the palace unexpected or uninvited. Everyone had to first send his ambassador to request an audience. He wanted to know the position of every head of state with regard to the Persian Empire and with regard to Farhastan. He let everyone understand that he was loyal to the Empire of Persia and particularly to its king, Rahman.

The former king of Persia, Harun Al-Rashid, had personally performed the coronation ceremony. It was a

remarkable event, never to be forgotten in the world. As Bousid wanted to please Soraya, and as both were of pure Arabian origin, they brought not only the Grand Mufti of Baghdad, but also the Ten Koran Elders. Bousid looked younger than King Rahman of Persia, despite his advanced age. Soraya, who had attracted princes and kings all her life, looked even younger than before, and no one understood why she had refused every marriage proposal, and yet had now chosen Bousid, an old man, unknown to the public.

Rabiya, the secretary of defense, who was well known to all, always spoke about Bousid with a lot of admiration. Already before the coronation, and even before they knew that Bousid was the son of General Omar, the rulers of neighboring countries respected Bousid. But after it became known to all that Bousid was the son of the general, the neighbors didn't dare challenge Farhastan anymore. Bousid had confused every king with his wisdom, firmness and kindness. With Bousid's new position, Farhastan, which had already a strong economy, gained more recognition, reputation and prestige. Every foreign country wanted to be allied with Farhastan, but Bousid kept calm and never said yes to anyone. He kept them in a state of anticipation. Every king desired to have him as a friend. The presence of Bousid in the political arena had strengthened Caliph Rahman of Persia. No one dared challenge Persia anymore for fear of its strongest ally, King Bousid Ben

Omar of Farhastan, who was so rich that he could supply any amount of money to Caliph Rahman for any military campaign. His presence alone brought stability and prosperity to the entire region. Bousid didn't forget the widows who produced the pottery and who trusted him with their merchandise. He invited all of them to come to Farhabad at the state's expense and to live there in prosperity and peace. A dozen widows accepted his invitation and moved to Farhabad with their families, but they did not want to live at the state's expense. They developed the ceramic industry and the rug industry, which became the city's best sources of revenue, along with tourism. The rest of the widows, those who could not move to Farhabad, received compensation from Bousid worth ten times the value of the goods, for their pottery and for their rugs.

One year after Bousid became king, it was the turn of Prince Mokhtar to wed Naziha.

Mokhtar didn't have any particular ambition. He established himself in quarters allocated to him and his new family.

Harun Al-Rashid's daughter was no longer in love with her husband Rahman. The caliph was too busy to take care of her. His responsibility as a king didn't leave him much time to spend with her, especially after she had given him five children. Rahman spent most of his time between travel and receptions. His day-to-day business

kept him very occupied. Harun Al-Rashid admired him for his seriousness and his hard work. For the wedding of Naziha and Mokhtar, Khayet was the first to arrive in Farhabad. Her children were already grown-up.

Mokhtar spent the entire year adapting himself to a new way of life, that of husband to his future wife. Naziha helped him transition to his new life. She was well educated and knew the etiquette of the palace. Meanwhile, he had learned the languages of the region and later became an excellent diplomat. He assisted his father in many audiences with heads of state. Despite the attractive women who came to the palace to court him, Mokhtar never betrayed Naziha. He loved her because of her education and her modesty. Mokhtar didn't want a pompous wedding. He was tired from his father's wedding and from the coronation ceremonies, which had lasted three months without a break. He saw so many princesses who had been invited to the ceremonies, but none had attracted him like his wife. He also had a great admiration for her sewing talents. He was always saying, "If her father was a bad man, it is not her fault; we have to judge her only on her own merit." He loved her very much, and Naziha loved him too. She had been prepared by Soraya for many years for this occasion. She had dreamt about him and had spent years waiting for him. She loved him without even seeing him, and in her view it was not important how he looked.

209

One day she said to the queen, "The most important thing for a man is that a woman loves him. Then, the man has no choice but to love her in return." Then she added, "Men think that they are the only ones who have the freedom to choose their partner. Men believe that a woman has no other choice but to accept her husband. But in reality it is the woman who chooses the man. The man is encouraged by the woman's positive reaction. In fact, the woman exercises her power towards the man, but she lets the man believe that he is the one who made the choice." Mokhtar eventually adjusted to his new life as a prince.

Chapter 15

The Difficult Case

No one could imagine that Bousid was not from a royal family. He was very successful in judging the people and the people loved him. Bousid had a great reputation as a judge and as a king. One day, King Bousid Ben Omar was presented with a very difficult case.

There was a man, a father of twelve children, who couldn't pay his rent anymore and owed two years' back rent to his landlord. One day the landlord went to the king with his tenant to complain. On their way they encountered a man with a stubborn donkey that didn't want to move from its place. The donkey was carrying a precious load. The owner of the donkey begged the passers-by for help. The tenant responded immediately to the request and tried to pull the donkey by its tail. He pulled so strongly that the tail of the donkey came off. The owner of the donkey was angry and wanted to hit the poor tenant, when the landlord stopped him and said, "Don't beat him. I am bringing him to the king. Come with me; he will have two cases instead of one." The owner of the donkey agreed and went with them holding

the donkey by the rope in one hand and the tail in the other.

The poor tenant was troubled to find himself with two cases on his hands. He walked without looking in front of him, and as he walked in despair he stepped on a baby whose parents had laid him down on the grass to enjoy the sunshine. The baby died instantly. The parents were furious and wanted to kill the poor tenant. The landlord intervened again and told the young couple, "Do not commit a crime. We are going to the king to have him judged. Join us; he will have to answer for three cases instead of one; he is already a dead man.

The couple joined the landlord and the owner of the donkey. The poor tenant walked listlessly and stumbled on every stone. After a while, he tripped on a big stone and tumbled down from a high rock. Deep under him was an old man surrounded by his five sons, sleeping in the shade of this high rock. The poor tenant fell on the old man's head and killed him instantly. The five sons were furious and wanted to kill him. Again, the landlord intervened and told the five sons the same story. The poor tenant didn't have any chance of getting out of this mess. His death was certain, said the landlord to the other plaintiffs.

When they entered the palace court, Bousid saw the tenant and recognized him. The tenant was an old friend, who had given his son two hundred camels at the time when Bousid needed them. At that time the tenant, who

used to be a rich man, had said to Mokhtar, Bousid's son, "Say to your father, 'God is generous!' One day Bousid will return me a favor if I need it." Bousid did not want to judge him immediately and waited until everyone was out of the court. It was almost night when the king called them to approach the bench.

The landlord took the lead and said to the judge, "Your Majesty, this man was a landlord himself, many years ago, and he should know what it means if a tenant does not pay his rent."

"To the point!" interrupted the king.

Then the landlord continued, "Very well. Next!"

The owner of the donkey approached the bench, and said while crying, "I have only this one donkey to work with, and this stupid man, instead of helping me, pulled the tail from my donkey. I asked him to push the donkey, not to pull."

"Next!" said the king.

The couple approached the bench, and the husband said, "My king, for many years my wife didn't have any children, and this year God blessed us with a boy. We were very happy, and then this crazy man stepped on the baby and killed him."

The king looked at the tenant with a faint smile and said, "Next! Now, what are you five men doing here?"

The oldest son approached the bench, while his four brothers stood behind him. He said, "My king, you know how precious parents are. We were sitting around our old father who was sleeping, when this heavy man comes from nowhere and falls on our father's head. Our poor dear father died instantly."

The king asked them, "How old was your father?"

The five men answered together, "Only one hundred years, Your Majesty."

The king looked at everyone and said, "Return in an hour. Let me think about all your cases."

Everyone waited patiently and hoped that the king would hang the tenant. Suddenly, the door opened wide and the king entered again with a severe expression on his face. The tenant's stomach turned over and he felt that his death was near. Then the king ordered them all out of the court hall and asked the guard to bring them in, case by case.

Then came the sentences. "Case number one", the judge said to the landlord, "give him another five years to pay his rent, and if he does not pay you, bring him back to me!"

When he heard the sentence, the landlord said, "Your Majesty, I pardon him. We will settle this case together. He is a good person after all."

Next, the donkey owner. "Your case is a very simple one. Give your donkey to the tenant, and he shall bring it back to you when the tail grows back."

When the donkey owner heard the sentence he said, as the landlord had said, "Your Majesty, I pardon him. He is a good man after all."

The third case was that of the young couple and the baby. "Your case is more than simple. Give him your wife, and he shall return her to you only if she becomes pregnant and will give birth to a baby boy."

The couple responded together, "Your Majesty, we too pardon him, as everyone has testified that he is a good man."

The fourth case, that of the five men and the father, followed. "Your case is an easy one." As the five men approached the bench, the judge ordered, "Your father was not so young, and his moment arrived while you were all surrounding him. That is a beautiful death. Now if you want to punish this man, then you should all jump on him from the top of the same rock until he is punished".

The five men were hesitant, as the top of the rock was very high, and they did not want to risk their lives, so together they responded, "Your Majesty, we pardon him too, as we heard from all the plaintiffs before us that this man was a good man. Therefore he should not die so young."

The plaintiffs left the palace court one by one, smiling as if they had just won the case. The brothers, who had seen the king for the first time, were very happy with this encounter and left the court smiling and praising the king's wisdom.

The court, which just a few minutes earlier had been full of people, was empty now, except for the tenant who was retained by the guards upon the king's instructions. The guards took him to the palace's bath and gave him fresh and rich-looking clothes. After a while, the tenant with the new clothes on, appeared like a prince and couldn't believe the luck he had had. He was full of joy and gratitude towards God. As he was about to leave the palace, the guards stopped him and told him that the king wanted to see him. The poor tenant was scared again that the king might have changed his mind. He followed the guards with a heavy heart. When he reached the king's room he looked like a king himself. In fact the clothes were royal. At the end of the majestic room, the king was waiting for him with many dignitaries. The king offered him a great reception.

The poor tenant was completely overwhelmed and could not understand what was going on. Then he addressed the king and said, "Your Majesty, there must be an innocent error. I am a poor man and do not belong in this beautiful place."

Then the king smiled and asked the poor tenant, "Do you not recognize me?"

The poor man, intimidated and with a frightened voice, replied, "No, Your Majesty."

The king approached him closer and said, "Take a good look at me and tell me if you recognize me."

The poor tenant looked at the king again and again, then he responded, "Your Majesty, I wish I knew you."

The king responded swiftly, "Of course you know me, my friend Jamil, the generous one, and the noble one."

Jamil, the tenant, responded with a laugh and continued, "The miserable one, and the naked one."

Then the king said to him, "You remember my son Mokhtar, to whom you gave two hundred camels?"

When the king mentioned Mokhtar and the camels, the poor Jamil replied, "Your Majesty, you mean my friend Bousid's son? Do you know him?"

Jamil was a little confused as he could not connect the camels, Bousid, who lived in another place, and now the king. It was too much for one single day and especially after a tiring journey.

The king answered, "Yes Jamil, your friend Bousid."

The tenant answered, "I wish I could find my friend Bousid; he is the only man I can trust."

The king smiled and said, "My dear friend Jamil, I am Bousid, and my son Mokhtar, whom you know, will arrive soon."

The tenant, completely seized with emotion, burst into tears.

The king kissed him and hugged him and said, "Do you remember, Jamil, the message you sent me through my son?"

Jamil remembered and said, "Tell your father, 'God is generous' and he shall return me a favor if I need it!"

Then the king said to him, "You recognized yourself that God is generous and that I should return you a favor if you needed it." Then he stopped for a moment and continued, "Could you choose a better day for a favor?"

Jamil answered, "No, this has been the most important day in my life. I thank our Lord for His generosity and justice. If I had been judged by another king, my head would not be on my shoulders by now."

After the short reception, the king took Jamil by his hand and entered another room where dinner was to be served. This time, in front of Queen Soraya, who was present, the king told him, "My friend Jamil, I proclaim you Mayor of the City of Farhabad." Then he turned to his wife Soraya and said, "My dear Soraya, do you agree with my decision?"

Soraya, who had listened to the entire story and was herself indirectly involved in it, said, "Of course, my king, let him bring his wife and his children here."

The king smiled and said, "You heard what the queen just said, go and bring your wife and your children here! The misery is over now, only good things await you. I will order my master builder to build you a house, so you can live with us in peace."

Soraya was very touched by this story, and she said to her husband, "I told you before, that during that dinner in your house, I saw greatness in your heart and later I also saw it in your son's heart. I am happy that I waited for you, and I am sure that my deceased husband will forgive me for having broken our vow.

Soraya became the great-grandmother of a boy called Tahar who inherited the kingdom, and in his name the city of Tehran was established. That's how the story of the caliph of Baghdad and king of Persia and Soraya the widow ends.

Postface

Here are a few verses from the original poem in their English translation and Arabic transliteration, which the author loves to recite from time to time. The numbers in front of the stanzas indicate the pages within the story where the particular scenes take place.

Legend:
a - as in apple, e - as in met, i = ee, j - as the "s" measure, gh - similar to "r"

63

Al-Rashid was walking to pass his time	Ar-Rashid agab ezman
He ran into a women of a noble family	Ordettoo toofla bint ness ekbar
Seeing her set his heart on fire	Ki mashafa shaalet fih naar
He had never seen one like her among women	Ma shaf she metla fenasswan

64

"Eyes of a gazelle,	"Ya ayoon eghezal
I want to marry you honestly	Nebdi nukhdek fel ahlal
And your reward will be a million	Naatik ajrek melioon mel
I will dress you in silk	Ou lebsek lahrir
And gold and precious stones"	Wel dheb wel moorjan"

221

64

"Rashid, please hear me out	"Ya Rashid, essma menni,
I was married to my cousin	Kunt mekhda weld ammi
Before my husband's death	Abel maimoot rajli
I gave him my handshake about men"	Al rajel atitoo laman"
(This is considered a holy vow)	

66

"Eyes of a gazelle,	"Ya ayoon eghezal
I will swiftly bring the judge to absolve you	Tawa enjiblek el qadi yevdilek
And the Ten Elders of the Koran"	Oo el ashra ntal Koran"

69

"Powerful Rashid	"Ya Rashid, ya sandid,
My words I will not take back	Klami mefish tawid
Even if they cut me in pieces with iron	Illu ntsatter bel ahdid
I will never betray the promise of the handshake"	Mankhunesh klem el aad"

72

Al-Rashid was fuming with rage	Ar-Rashid traad fi raada kwia
He went to the wazir and told him,	Umsha lel oozir, qaloo,
"My wazir, advise me,	"Ya oozir daber aliya
What should I do with this lady?"	Esh ekoun fi bint eflan"

73

"Al-Rashid, this is a small request	"Ya Rashid, hadi talba zrira
We will falsely accuse her son	Tawa nedlemoo weldha
Saying he insulted the religion of the sultan"	Kooloo keiloo seb din el sultan"

74

They grabbed him and in the dark jail they put him	Hazoohoo, oo fel habs edlam hatoohoo
And what's more, in iron they shackled him	Oo zadoo bel ahdid katfoohoo
When his mom heard it, she said,	Semat mimtoo kalet
"My poor son, they falsely accused him"	"Ya naari ala oolidi, dalmoohoo,"

77

"Rashid, make me a public judgment	"Ya Rashid ameli khtiya shaariya
In front of the people and the judges"	Qbalet el mezless oo diwan"

78

"Your son's case is a tiny matter	"Hooeyjet weldek hooeyjat zrar
Bring me one thousand and one female camels	Jibli meniug elf naga oo naga
Aged of one year and mixed in all colors"	Am wahad, mkhaltin kool elwan."

81

"Go to Sir Bousid el Hallali	"Emshi le Si Bousid Le Hallali
When he will see you	Ki shoufek
He will not let you down"	Mei khalish ibik"

129

"My son, a lady came	"Ya oolidi, jaat mra
He offered her dinner and to a thousand camel drivers	Ashaha, oo asha elf znad m'aha
	Book ihab alakhlaha
Your father wants our ruin	Oo ihabek tootleb al jiran."
And wants you to beg the neighbors"	

129

"Mother, I came back sweating	"Ya mimti, ana jit fi arga
And you added fire to my heart	Oo inti zitni fi galbi harga
I will mount my mare right away	Tawa nerkeb al zarga
And bring back everything as it was"	Oo n'rood kol makan"

130

When he saw her, he said,	Ki mashafha kal,
"Cursed be the devil	"Intallah al eshitan
The generous give precious stones when their value is the highest	El krim yaati eteber oo illaghla
And the stingy do not even give a drop of water from their goatskin.	Oo larmaz sharba ma men gerba tkidha
My father gave one thousand and one camels	Baba aata elf naga oo naga
And I add the mare I'm sitting on, on top."	Oo ana el zarga meltahti zidha"